Will-O Wisp

Of Niagara Falls

By Lady Laindora

Will-O Wisp of Niagara Falls is a work of fiction by author Lady Laindora A.K.A. Sue Raymond. The people and places are the work of fiction or used fictitiously and are not related to any person alive or dead.

Upon Eagle's Wings, Malachi Ink Publishing

516 East Park Avenue, Des Moines, Iowa 50315

Excerpt from 'Voids' by LaVina Vanorny-Barcus by permission

ISBN: 978-0-9982942-3-0

Dedication

Thank you to everyone who made this endeavor possible, most of all to the Lord. For the Lord makes everything possible and without Him nothing is possible.

You can find other novels written by Lady Laindora / Sue Raymond at www.amzn.to/1u92UUj

www.books2read.com/ap/nzwk28/Sue-Raymond

ACKNOWLEDGMENTS

I wish to acknowledge my writing team Davenport Writes, LLC, which is essential to the publication of my novels. And a heartfelt thank you to our departed team member, Dan.

Lady Laindora

CHAPTER 1

The fog was a thick gray swirling mass which shrouded the Maid of the Mist 3. Twenty-three-year-old Ongwaterohiathe Whitehorse coiled the rope before he stored it in the aft stern locker in the pilot tower. His jet black hair fell across his forehead as he left the pilot tower and headed down the stairs toward the gangplank He was glad this day was finally over. If he hurried, Ongwaterohiathe would be in time for the first reading by the Iowa Indie Author Group at the Theater Loft in the heart of Elmwood Village before the play of *'Because of Me'* by J.C. Hamm.

The clean deck lay empty after being flooded with blue plastic poncho covered bodies as they crowded the railing for the premier spot to capture the particular moment on a photograph to commemorate their visit to the falls.

Ongwaterohiathe glanced over at the roaring falls as he was about to leave the ship. The fog blanketed the falls but failed to cover the growl of the falls drumming in his head. He turned to wave goodnight to the pilot when Ongwaterohiathe caught a glimpse of a slim Kanyenkehaha woman at the bow railing.

Her long raven hair was braided in a waterfall twist into a mermaid braid darkened by the thick mist. His sister had tried for months to master that particular braiding technique without success. The woman turned her head toward Ongwaterohiatha as the fog swallowed her.

Ongwaterohiathe ran back to the bow searching for her. He could not see her anywhere. Ongie snatched the life preserver as he combed the turbulent water for any sign of her. She appeared thirty feet down the river for a mere moment.

Ongie launched his six-foot-four-inch frame over the railing, using it for an extra foot boost. As the torrent river closed over his head, he heard, *"Ongie No*! She's not real!"

Ongie's temples hammered as he tried to rise. A gentle hand pushed him back down on the pillow as a cold cloth covered his broad forehead and eyes Ongie could hear the distant falls roar as it rumbled along. It vibrated all around him. He pulled the towel from his eyes and focused dimly on the ornate glass dome over him holding back the turbulent waters of the Niagara River.

"No, no it can't be," he struggled against the gentle embrace.

"Sh-sh everything is all right. She can't find you here."

"Can't find me, who is she? The last thing I remember, I jumped into the river to rescue a young Kanyenkehaha woman that fell overboard. Is she safe? Did someone rescue her?" Ongie's strength depleted and sank once again against the pillow.

"There is no need for concern over that one. She can never die." The cloth covered his eyes once more.

Ongie woke to the stench of a hospital room. His eyes crossed under the harsh light making hazy shadows of the hospital personnel. A shadow glided to the end of his bed. Ongie focused harder as he cleared his throat to gain the shadow's attention.

"Well Mr. Whitehorse, it is nice to meet you finally. I have been waiting for a long time to do so."

Mesa Soyok Wuhti appeared at the foot of the hospital bed. "I do not know how you escaped us at the falls, however; there will be no escaping from me here." She brushed back the long straggly black hair with the jagged-edged knife covered with blood. Her wide eyes stared as fangs appeared at the corners of thin lips.

The knife drew back over her head ready to be plunged into Ongie's neck as Mesa Soyok Wuhti climbed over the foot of the bed.

Ongie could not move. His eyes riveted on the snarled face shining with glee over her apparent victory.

Mesa Soyok Wuhti crawled over his body, scratching and clawing the thin cover over Ongie. Her body twitched as she came up his chest. Her foul breath gagged the air out of Ongie's lungs. She drew herself erect upon Ongie's rib cage. The knife held high above her head then it plunged down toward his throat, "*Soyoka-u-u-u!*"

CHAPTER 2

"Ahahaha ah hee!" Ongie bolted straight up in the hospital bed. Sweat poured from every pore of his body. He strained to draw air into his lungs.

Randy jumped from his chair to the side of the bed and grabbed his friend by the shoulders. "Ongie you're alright, man. You're safe."

Ongie focused in on Randy's face as he grasped for Randy's shoulder. "Did you see her? Did she cut me? Her breath was so foul I couldn't breathe."

"Ongie who are you talking about? There hasn't been anyone in here for over two hours except for me."

"Mesa Soyok Wuhti."

"Mesa Soyok Wuhti? The monster woman, your grandfather, used to scare us with when we were kids? Man, you must have hit your head along with trying to swallow the whole river last night. We thought we lost you for a while. You kept bobbing like a cork through the foam and fog then we lost track of you. We found you two miles downriver. The life preserver caught on a low-hanging tree branch. Somehow you were able to wedge your head and shoulder through the center. Otherwise, you would have been a goner, man." Randy patted Ongie's shoulder as a wide grin crossed his bronzed face.

They turned as the door opened to a young female intern.

She smiled as she looked up from the chart, "Ah Mr. Whitehorse I am glad you have joined the living. It was touch and go for a while. We pumped quite a bit of water from your lungs and stomach. You will be our guest for a while to make sure pneumonia does not develop in your lungs." She came over and ran a thermometer across his forehead. Then she wrapped a blood pressure cuff around his arm and started pumping away on the bulb.

Ongie winced as the cuff tightened on his bruised arm. It felt like the intern was sawing his arm off. After she checked his blood pressure, she placed the stethoscope on his chiseled chest listened for any rattle in the lungs then listened to his heart. She smiled at the results.

"Well Mr. Whitehorse, everything sounds fine. If everything stays the same, you will not have that extended hospital stay after all. You should be able to leave by five tonight. I will check back in on you before noon to make the decision."

Randy slapped Ongie on the back, "Hey that will be great. We will be able to make tonight's performance of 'Because of Me.' Your dip in the Niagara made us miss Jordyn Meryl's reading. Remember, she's the author that writes with spice. I had everything planned, go to the reading, pick up a hottie, see the play, wine and dine my date and then reap the rewards of all my hard work."

Ongie shook his head. "You're always on the prowl for the next conquest."

CHAPTER 3

They stood in the line that stretched around the block waiting for the Theater doors to open at six-thirty. Randy's five-foot-eleven-inch muscular frame twisted in frustration at being so far back in line. He shoved his hands deeper into his pockets. He glowered at Ongie standing to his right. Randy craned his neck to see if the line was moving.

"Randy the line isn't going to go any faster just because you want it to." Ongie shook his head. "If you wanted to get here sooner you should've brought me a clean set of clothes like I asked you then I wouldn't have had to run home first."

"It wouldn't have hurt you to wear the clothes you had at the hospital." Randy huffed and leaned over trying to see around the corner.

Ongie gave Randy a slight shove with his foot. Randy stumbled toward the street and the sizeable stagnant puddle in the gutter. Randy caught himself before falling face first into the mire. His foot and hand sank in the leaf muck.

"Damn it Ongie. What did you do that for?" Randy shook his hand and foot trying to get rid of the clinging muck. "Now I'm going to smell like rotten leaf mold."

Ongie gave him a smirk, "Now you know what my clothes smelt like. There is no way I was coming stinking of muck from the bottom of the Niagara."

Randy gave him a sneer, "Keep my place in line. I'm going to have to run back to the car which is parked five blocks away and get my work boots. At least they will be dry." He ran off leaving sloshy footprints in his wake on the sidewalk.

Two teenage girls giggled and slid into Randy's place as they made eyes at Ongie. He gave them a quick smile then turned around so not to be tempted by the gorgeous jailbait behind him. The line started moving quickly then stopped suddenly. The girls bumped up against him, and Ongie felt a quick grope on his firm rear as one of the girls mumbled, "Oh sorry," as the other one giggled. The first girl gave her a quick little punch in the arm as the line started again.

Randy came back to find the line was five feet from the door and Ongie nowhere in sight. He let out a billingsgate as he handed his ticket to the usher.

The extra-large guard stepped up behind the usher. "Is there going to be a problem here?" His granite jaw jetted out daring Randy to take a swing.

Randy hung his head, mumbling no as he took his ticket stub and darted through the door into the lobby. It was wall-to-wall people. Randy hopped up and down trying to locate Ongie's six-foot-four-inch frame in the swirling mass. Ongie was nowhere which meant he already was in the reading parlor. Randy ground his teeth. Ongie knew he had to be up close to get all the books his family demanded.

He weaved his way through the mass of bodies towards the reading parlor. Halfway there he ran into a solid wall of people. There was not even an inch of space at the wall. He worked his way to the right to try to find a space to wedge through. He reached the wall seeing it covered with potted plants. Randy saw his chance and threaded his way through the tiny area around the pots.

He felt a squeeze on his rear as he emerged from the plants. And he turned to see the teenage girl smile as she slid her hand up and placing a finger through her plump lips, making a popping sound as she slowly removed it. Randy glided over to her, gazing down into sea green eyes. "Oh, sweet thing if you were only twenty-one I would so enjoy returning that grope."

She batted her long lashes at him as she flashed him her ID. "Come on I'm eighteen."

Randy flashed a toothy grin. "Honey that phony ID wouldn't get you into Kiddyland. Come back and look me up in say five years." He turned and threaded his way through the crowd and squeezed into the reading parlor. He spotted Ongie down in front as author LaVina Vanorny-Barcus was finishing her reading section from her novel *'Voids.'*

"Captain Lane noted the reading on the ship's gauges about fifteen minutes after their departure. Suddenly, he noticed the nautical miles per hour were decreasing in small increments, but nonetheless, steadily decreasing. He stood up to see the water in front of the ferry a little closer. The water was coming towards the ferry with a lot of force. Normally the current in this part of the lake was crossing side to side. He quickly checked his instruments and then scanned the horizon to check his position. Confused, he pushed the throttle forward on the control panel and heard the engine respond with a loud growl, but still, the ferry was not advancing as he expected it would.

Captain Lane looked at the anemometer which measures the wind speed. The wind was only ten mph, not enough to affect their progress." She stopped and looked over at the other set of doors on the far wall. A man with a headset was signaling to her. LaVina turned back to the audience. "Well, it's time to seat for the play. We all thank you for coming and hope that you have a wonderful time reading the novels you have purchased and please enjoy the play." She gave a slight bow and returned to the tables behind her where her fellow authors Jordyn Meryl, J.C. Hamm and Sue Raymond waited for her so that they could leave by the stage door.

Randy pushed and shoved against the flow of people trying to reach the group before they escaped the mob of fans still mingling around the authors. He was about there when he ran aground against the granite chest of the guard he had encountered at the front door.

The guard placed a beefy paw on Randy's chest and gave him a shove backward. "Where's your VIP

Pass, buddy? No one gets past this point without a VIP pass."

"But I need to buy books. I was sent specifically for that reason. Please just let me get the books I need, and I will be out of your hair."

The guard brushed his hand over his shaven head. "There's no hair to be in, turn around and go to your seat for the play or you're out on your ear. The choice is yours, Mack." He ground his right fist into his left hand as he advanced towards Randy.

Randy turned tail and beat a hasty retreat following the remaining group back into the lobby. It took fifteen minutes to gravitate through the main auditorium doors then he had to pat himself down because he forgot where he placed his ticket stub to show the usher. Randy stumbled down the darkened aisle bumping and elbowing patrons on his way to his seat. He fell into the seat beside Ongie as the curtain rose. The actress playing fifteen-year-old Jessica watched from the upstairs window as the actor stumbled from the truck into the house.

Randy leaned over and whispered loudly in Ongie's ear. "Thanks a lot. That stunt you pulled cost me too much time, so I wasn't able to get the books. Clan Mother is going to have me flayed."

A loud hiss behind them stopped any further conversation. Randy slumped into his chair with his head on his upraised hand. He shoved Ongie's arm off the chair arm with his elbow, grumbling throughout the whole play.

The play received a standing ovation at the conclusion. There were three curtain calls before the audience let the cast leave.

Ongie bent down and pulled out two full stacks of books from under his chair. He gloated at Randy's shocked expression as he turned and followed the crowd out of the theater. Randy just stood there with his mouth hanging open.

CHAPTER 4

Ongie put the sacks in the trunk and started to close the trunk lid when an eerie feeling he was being watched washed over him. He glanced around the darkened street. Elongated shadows covered the boulevard, but there was no one lurking among them that he could tell. He chided himself for being so jittery. He walked around to the driver side of the car. He fished in his jean pocket for his keys. As he slid the key in the door lock, a hand clamped down on his shoulder.

Ongie spun around, his fists raised to ward off the pending attack. Randy burst out laughing. "Man, you should see the terror on your face. Whatsamatter Ongie? Is Mesa still looking to put you in her basket to fatten you up before she cuts your head off for her stew?"

Ongie gave Randy a shove. "Knock it off Naulowa! It's not funny. That nightmare felt real. I can still smell her foul breath on my face."

"Ah, little Ongwaterohiathe is shivering right down to his toes over a child's bedtime character. Are you going to start crying and pee down your leg like you did when your grandpa jumped out at you at the campfire? And I do not use Naulowa for my name anymore."

"Then stop acting like an adder, and it was you, not me that peed down his leg that night." Ongie opened the door and slid in behind the wheel. "Stop puffing your cheeks in and out and get in the car. I will treat you to a late supper at St. Regis casino."

Randy hopped over the hood of the car and impatiently waited for Ongie to unlock the passenger door. Randy slid in, slamming the door shut. He started drumming on the dashboard as Ongie started the car.

"Would you please stop drumming long enough to buckle up, so we can get there by midnight?"

Randy stopped long enough to buckle in. "It's not going to take us till midnight to reach the casino. Oh, wait, Yertle, the Turtle, is behind the wheel."

Ongie just smirked and put the car in reverse, backing out of the parking space and sped off toward St. Regis reservation. A tall scrawny woman stepped out of the shadows watching the car taillights disappear. The bloody jagged knife tapped the side of her leg in rhythm with Randy's drumming on the dashboard.

Will-O Wisp

CHAPTER 5

THE casino was in full swing by the time they arrived. Rayen Whitehorse was at the hostess stand as they threaded their way up to the station. Randy swung Rayen up in his arms. "Hi gorgeous, did you miss me? You sure feel good." He let her slide down him enjoying every moment of her curves touching his body. Ongie turned and started playing the nearest nickel slot machine.

Rayen gave Randy a quick peck on the cheek and pried his hands off her. "Randy stop this, this is my place of business. You just can't come barging in anytime you want." She turned her back on him and greeted the group of ladies that came in. "Good evening, thank you for joining us tonight. Have you placed a prior reservation, or do you wish to be put on the list and sit in the bar section while you wait?"

The short, stout lady with long dark hair crowned with white smiled. "We have a reservation under the name of Raymond."

Rayen looked down her list. "Yes. Here it is Sue Raymond, table for four." She picked up four menus. "Right this way. We placed you in the corner booth for privacy, but you still can see the floor show fine."

Randy stared at the group walking away. Rayen came back and picked up two menus and motioned for them to follow her. She snaked her way through the full tables. Randy stayed right against her with Ongie bringing up the rear. "Randy, I take it by your happy expression, you were able to get the entire list of books Clan Mother sent you after tonight." Rayen purred over her shoulder.

Randy stopped short, and Ongie ran into him. "Signal when you're going to pull up short, Randy. I was almost the main course for this table." Ongie turned and apologized to the couple he almost fell on.

Rayen stared at Randy. "Don't tell me you screwed up and didn't get the books. You had one thing to do today, and you bungled it?"

"It wasn't my fault. Ongie pushed me in the mud, and by the time I got my shoes changed and came back, the place was too packed for me to reach the sales table."

"Randy with you, it's just one excuse after another. This way you will never be elected to the Council as Sachem. How are you going to impress Clan Mother if you can't even do a small assignment like this?"

Randy pointed over to the corner booth. "Don't count me out just yet. I'm still in the running." He plucked the menu from Rayen's hand and strutted off towards the corner booth.

Ongie patted Rayen on the shoulder as he gave her a quick peck on the cheek. "Don't worry Sis. I'll keep him reigned in. Those ladies are the authors we went to see tonight." Then he slowly followed Randy to the booth.

Randy sauntered up to the table and slid into the booth next to Jordyn. She leaned back and gave him the once over, glancing at the shocked expression of the rest of the group before turning back to the stunning bronze young hunk of a man sitting beside her with a gorgeous smile. "Well just make yourself at home." She turned resting her elbow on the table with chin in hand.

"Thank you for allowing me to intrude on your evening. I'm pleased to be able to join the four lovely and talented ladies I have ever met." Randy picked up

Jordyn's hand, caressing it before kissing her fingers as he slowly withdrew his hand from hers.

Sue smirked. "Well, the honey covered bull has been served. Now young man, kindly tell us what you have on your mind without the second serving of molasses."

Jordyn took a sip of her red beer. "Mind your own business, Sue. I saw him first." Then turned back to Randy. "Now handsome, just because I write love stories with a little bit of spice doesn't mean a hunky gorgeous little boy barging into adult conversation spouting crap can sway my brain. Just what is it that you want from us?" Jordyn batted her eyes as the corner of her mouth curled up into a crooked smile.

Everyone burst out into laughter as Randy squirmed uncomfortably and stammered, "I er I er I er I'm," he started to rise.

Jordyn grabbed his hand and pulled him back down beside her. She raised his hand and blew softly over it before she kissed it and joined the rest laughing. "Sit still kiddo and tell us what is on your mind. You must want to relay something important to us to interrupt our late-night dinner conversation."

Randy turned redder than his scarlet shirt. "I -hm -er," was all he could get out as he slumped down in the seat.

"Sue, Jordyn, stop tormenting the boy. Can't you see you frustrated him beyond his endurance?" LaVina smiled at Randy. "Let's start by introducing ourselves. We are J.C. Hamm, Sue Raymond, Jordyn Meryl and I am LaVina Vanorny-Barcus. But I have the feeling you already know this. May we please have your name? It would make it easier to carry on this conversation."

Ongie arrived at the table. "Please excuse the intrusion of my now tongue-tied friend here. I am Ongwaterohiathe Whitehorse. My friends call me Ongie, and this here is Naulowa Graystone."

"Randy- my name is Randy Graystone. I don't go by Naulowa." Randy's tongue finally came untied. He straightened up in the booth.

"Randy here was given a special request by our Clan Mother to buy all of your books for our library on the reservation." He smiled.

"However, Ongwaterohiathe thought it would be funny to shove me in a mud puddle, and by the time I changed my shoes, I lost my place in line and wasn't able to supplant the three thousand people in front of me to reach the sales table before it closed." Randy shot back.

J.C. tilted her head, "Clan Mother?"

"Yes, may I sit down, and I will explain." Ongie inquired.

"Please do, we would like to hear more about your Clan Mother and the reservation. Are you talking about the reservation here at St. Regis?" LaVina smiled as they made room for Ongie in the booth as Randy scowl at his intrusion on what he considered his territory.

Sue smile. "Which tribe of Iroquois do you both belong to?"

"That's very perceptive of you Ms?" Ongie turned to the smile.

"Mrs. Sue Raymond, you may call me Sue."

Randy jumped in, "Most white people have no idea that there is more than one tribe of Iroquois on the reservation."

Sue leaned her elbow on the table and rested her chin on the back of her hand. "Yes, us white people do have some intelligence to know how to look things up on the Internet before coming, so we do not look and sound like total idiots."

"Sue, rein in your claws. I'm sure he didn't mean anything by it." Jordyn pointed a warning finger at Sue.

Sue broke into a small laugh. "Ah come on Jordyn, I haven't sliced up anyone to ribbons in over three weeks now. My claws are getting dull from non-use. A little tender flesh is just what they need to make them razor-sharp again." She flicked one long fingernail under the other making a small snapping sound.

Ongie and Randy gave each other a quick sideward glance.

"Sue, stop! They are going to think that you are serious." J.C. cut in.

A broad smile stretched across Sue's face. "I'm sorry, I couldn't help myself. We had just been talking about one of the Native American legends to see how it would work out as the villain in a horror story."

Ongie smiled back. "What legend would that be?"

"I believe Sue said her name was Mesa Soyok Wuhti." LaVina sipped her wine.

Ongie made a small jerk at the mention of the name. Only Randy saw it. "Mesa Soyok Wuhti would make a great villain. Even some adults still cower at the mention of her name. Don't you Ongie?"

Ongie looked like he could rip that smart-aleck grin off Randy's face. "Now is not the time to bring that up." He hissed under his breath.

"Sure, it is Ongie. Old Ongie here just had a run in with Mesa just the other day. He swore she was crawling up upon his bed ready to chop his head off. He woke up screaming his lungs out. If I hadn't been there to calm him down, he would've woken the whole ward up with his screaming."

"Ward? What were you guys doing in a ward? And by the way, what kind ward would that have been?" Jordyn shot a wary eye over at LaVina.

"I was in the hospital from a near drowning in the Niagara River." Ongie quickly explained.

LaVina placed a sympathetic hand on Ongie's arm. "Oh, you poor boy, are you all right? What happened?"

"You don't want waste your time on that." Ongie tried to change the subject. "How about if you join me out on the dance floor while you wait for your dinner to arrive?"

LaVina took his hand, "Sure, why not."

They passed Rayen on the way to the dance floor. Ongie threw his dinner order over his shoulder at her as he swept LaVina into his arms swaying to the music. Randy took J.C. by the hand, pulling her to the dance floor as not to be outdone by Ongie. He whizzed by Rayen and told her to put him down for a steak, rare, on Ongie's tab. The tempo had been in full swing and rose to a fever pitch before the band ended the music.

A lady stepped to the microphone and announced it was time for a line dance. Quick as a wink, Sue, and Jordyn found themselves along with the rest of the group out on the dance floor, high-stepping to *Doctor, Doctor*.

CHAPTER 6

They swept through *'Reggae Cowboy'* and *'Something in the Water'* before J.C. broke free to go to the restroom. She walked into the stall, and as she placed the lock bar in place, the air turned frigid. J.C.'s breath came out in puffs of frosty white as she heard the restroom door open and close. A chill ran down J.C.'s spine as it filled her with dread. Then there was a horrible cackle as the temperature dropped to sub-zero.

"I can smell you Christian. I know you're in here. Your fear is breaking down the hedge God has placed around your group. This hedge may protect you, but it won't protect the Iroquois. I have claimed them for my own." J.C. heard metal being dragged across the vanity top as Mesa Soyok Wuhti drew nearer to the stall where J.C. was.

J.C. stepped back; her legs bumped into the toilet. She stepped up on the toilet trying to make it harder to find her. J.C. did her best to get into a fighting stance from her black belt training. If this person wanted a fight, J.C. would oblige them. J.C.'s breath now hung in the air in delicate ice crystals. She could see the elongated shadow arrive under the door as the door handle shook.

"I've got you now." The cackle boomed as the tip of the bloody knife slipped through the crack between the door and the stall wall. J.C. said a quick prayer of protection as the blade started to raise the lock bar. J.C. balanced on the balls of her feet ready to spring when the door opened.

As the lock latch came free, the knife disappeared, and J.C. sprang out the door, giving her fiercest karate scream as Sue went into the restroom.

Sue drew back in shock at J.C.'s sudden appearance. J.C. quickly glanced around. The bathroom was empty except for the two of them. "Sue, that wasn't funny. Where did you hide the knife so quickly?"

"I should say not. Why did you jump out of the stall like that?" Sue cocked her head. "What knife? What are you talking about? I don't have a knife."

J.C. shook her head. "When I went into the stall, the air turned frigid and someone was dragging a knife across the vanity as they told me they could smell my fear and the hedge that God placed around our group wouldn't protect the Iroquois from them. Then they gave a horrible cackle and slid what looked like a bloody knife through the slot and unlocked the stall door. I jumped out, and only you were here."

Sue slid her arm around J.C.'s shoulder. "Hmm, it was cold when I first came in. The temperature is nice and warm now. No one left right before I came in. The Lord does say where two or three are gathered in His name; He will be there also." She gave J.C. an extra hug. Her upper lip twisted slightly, "Are you sure Jordyn or LaVina didn't spike your Coke with wine or red beer?" She tried to lighten the mood. "You know you almost scared the pee right out of me when you jumped out at me. I came to see if you were alright and to tell you they served our food since you were taking so long."

J.C. pulled back. "What do you mean so long? I've only been here five minutes."

"J.C., look at your watch. You've been in here for forty-five minutes."

Will-O Wisp

CHAPTER 7

They returned to the table and joined back in the conversation as they ate their meal.

"Yes, the Mohawk nation called themselves Kanyenkehaha, which means people of kayenke. Kayneke means flint or crystal." Randy puffed out his chest as he drummed his fingers on the table.

"And if my research is correct, the tribe is ruled by the Clan Mother and Sachems who are male, are underneath her in the pecking order." Sue wiped the corner of her mouth with her napkin.

Randy drew his mouth down into a pout.

"That's correct Sue." Ongie smiled. "The Iroquois people call themselves Haudenosaunee which means people of the longhouse. Our clan has a matriarch society structure, divided into three clans the turtle, the bear, and the wolf. I would love it if all of you considered being my guest at our annual Ironwork Festival tomorrow. We are trying something new this year. We are combining the Festival with the Pow Wow. You would be coming as my special guests so there would be no charge. I do have an alternative motive for asking you to come."

"What would that motive be?" J.C. asked.

The corner of Ongie's mouth turned up, "I propose that you have a reading of an excerpt from your novels for the public along with a book signing. It would be a win, win situation. This way you can sell your books to make up for the donation of books maybe you would give to the library? There is no cost for the table rental. That is if you are all agreeable to it. There are eleven events along with lots of food, storytelling from the False Face Sociality."

"The False Face Sociality?" LaVina looked puzzled.

Ongie smiled as he leaned forward, setting his glass down, "The False Face Sociality is the healing group of the clan. They wear a grotesque wooden mask to frighten away evil spirits that are believed to cause illness. My grandfather is one of the best and can tell the most horrendous stories of evil spirits that can keep you awake for weeks."

"Yeah, Ongie should know. He still has to have a nightlight to make sure Mesa isn't lurking in the darkened corners, waiting to cart him off in her basket." Randy smarted off and rubbed his shin from where Ongie kicked it.

"Mesa Soyok Wuhti is a Hopi legend, isn't she?" Sue picked at her food. "How do you know about her?"

"Ongie's grandfather brought the story of Mesa and her Katsinas back with him when he was in his twenty's. He used to tell us about how she would catch bad children and put them in her basket. Then would fatten them up for her stew pot." Randy gave a crooked smile at Ongie.

"What is Katsinas?" J.C. looked over at Ongie.

"Katsinas are ogres that protect Mesa," Sue added. "The Ironworker Festival and Pow Wow is Tomorrow?"

"Yes." Ongie took a drink of water.

"So, would that mean both you are ironworkers that work high up in the skyscrapers walking the steel I-beams?" LaVina sipped her wine.

"I'm the ironworker. I'm the one who rivets the beams together. Ongie here is afraid of heights, so he works as the captain's co-pilot on the Maid of the Mist." Randy flipped his thumb over at Ongie.

"What about the books you were to buy, Randy? What were the titles?" Jordyn changed the subject.

Randy fished in his jeans pocket and produced a crumpled wad of paper. He smoothed it out on the table to remove enough wrinkles to be readable. He handed it to Jordyn, then chugged his beer down and raised his glass to catch the waitress' eye that he wanted a refill.

Jordyn glanced down the list and passed it to LaVina. "It looks like from what I can decipher Randy was supposed to buy four of each of our books for the library. What do you say if we donate half of them and let Randy purchase the rest?" LaVina looked at the list and passed it on.

"I'm in for that plus it would be great to attend the festival. We could personalize the autographed books to the library. I would love to record some of the stories for reference for future novels. Ongie, do you think your grandfather would agree to allow me to record him while he's telling the stories?" Sue passed the list to J.C..

A broad smile broke out across Ongie's face. "Sue, I hope you have at least a hundred recording CDs along with nothing to do for the next three weeks. My grandfather will talk your arm off and not stop until your mind is buried under three feet of stories. You will have no trouble getting enough reference material for a complete series."

Sue returned his smile, "Wonderful; I love listening to storytellers." She turned to the group, "So do we accept Ongie's kind offer to be his guests tomorrow?"

The answer was a unanimous yes and Ongie swept Sue up on the dance floor for a slow waltz. Randy was not going to be outdone by Ongie, and LaVina found herself swept around the dance floor in Randy's strong arms.

Although firmly held in Ongie's warm, strong embrace, Sue felt a frigid blast of air sweep across the dance floor as a young Kanyenkehaha woman walked onto the dance floor. She tilted her head glancing across the dance floor and locked onto Ongie's broad shoulders. Her dress shimmered in the moving lights as it clung to her stunning figure. She licked her plush lips as she drew her long, glistening black hair over her ear and headed toward them. She glided through the dancers as if she was on sliding on ice.

She smiled as she received admiring glances from all the men but glares from their partners as they pulled them from her path. The closer she came, the more frigid the air around Sue became.

Sue glanced up at Ongie to see if he also felt the change in temperature. There was no sign on Ongie's face that he felt any change. Dread covered Sue in a cocoon of suffocating trepidation. She drew a deep breath as she prayed for a hedge of protection against the pending terror.

A second later, a petite young lady with a perky chestnut pixie haircut tapped Sue on the shoulder. "May I cut in?" She smiled as she held out her hand for Ongie to take it. Sue handed Ongie off to her, and they twirled away as the Kanyenkehaha woman drew five feet from them.

A stoic stare washed over the woman's face as she watched Ongie twirl out of her reach. She turned to find Sue had retreated to the safety of the booth. Seeing that both people escaped her grasp, she turned her attention to Randy who had not taken his eyes off her since she stepped on the dance floor.

Try as she might, LaVina could not divert Randy's attention away from the woman. The woman slid her hand down the length of her body as she swayed seductively with the music. Dancers gave way as she slithered towards Randy.

She slid right up, molding her body against his back. She wrapped her arms under his and ran her hands up Randy's chest, dragging her fingernail across the base of his neck, leaving a small red welt in its wake.

Randy dropped LaVina's hands and turned on his heels to allow the woman to mold her body against him again as he took her hand and slid his hand across her back stopping right above her butt. He nestled her face close to his as his lips brushed across her cheek. "Mmmm baby, where have you been all my life? Your looks have lit a volcanic eruption in my soul." His hand now explored her luscious bottom as murmurs of desire bubbled out of his lips.

She laughed and tossed her head allowing her hair to fly out in an arch as they flew around the dance floor. The other dancers gave way as they flew by. Soon they were the only ones on the dance floor. Randy's desire grew with each swirl across the floor.

Ongie stood against the bar with his arms wrapped around the petite lady's waist, watching Randy sweep by with pure bliss plastered across his face. "Boy, Randy is flying high! He is in seventh heaven right now." Ongie smiled. "By the way my name is Ongie. What name graces you?"

"My name is Will-O. If you have any sway with your friend, we need to find a way to break this up before it's too late." She drew his arms closer around her as a shiver ran through her slim body.

Ongie pulled her tighter, "Why would I do that? Randy is having the time of his life. Randy would never forgive me if we did something to stop this. Why would you want to? What do you know about her that would make it necessary to break this up?" He smiled as he turned her toward him.

Will-O turned and placed a soft hand on Ongie's chest. "Wherever that one goes, only heartache follows. I can only protect one of you at a time, and I chose you."

Ongie laughed, "What do I need protection from that you can do which I cannot do for myself? Willow is a beautiful name."

The only answer he received was a very concerned gaze. He could not resist it. "Okay let's go rescue Randy from seventh heaven. You do know, Willow; he will hate me for the next five years because of this." He snagged her hand and started toward the twirling couple.

The closer they came to Randy, the faster the woman begged Randy to go. Her face drew down into a scowl as they drew near. She stopped the swirl and pulled on Randy's arm, "Come on love, I will show you the best night you will ever have. Come."

Ongie reached out and snagged Randy's arm, "Come on Randy, you need to go get the books Clan Mother sent you to buy for the library. They are not going to wait all night for you. You know what will happen if you show up and do not have the books for Clan Mother. Get her number and call her later." He pulled harder.

Randy turned from Ongie to the woman. "Wait here for a moment. I will not be long. I just have to buy a few books then I will be right back."

"If you go, I will not be here when you return. I wait for no one for my fun. I thought you were a man. Now I see you for what you truly are, only a little boy playing at being an adult." She taunted as she threw glaring daggers at Will-O.

Will-O stood firm holding Ongie's hand. She reached out with her other hand and placed it on Randy's arm beside Ongie's hand. The Kanyenkehaha woman flung her hand off Randy as if a bolt of lightning had stricken her.

The woman stepped back as she hissed, "This round goes to you. However, I succeed in my objectives. You are just a minute bump in the road. No one can have what I have chosen for my own. And this delicious one is mine, for my collection. You cannot guard them both all the time." She blew a kiss to Randy. "I will see you later; love, when you grow a bigger set." She laughed as she glided from the dance floor into the crowd.

The Kanyenkehaha woman sauntered up to the bouncer. She pulled him to her as her lips latched onto his, drinking deeply. When she allowed him to come up for air, she smiled, "You'll do for now." Her arm snaked into the crook of his arm and led him off into the crowd.

Randy watched her disappear then turned to Ongie. He gave him a small shove out of the way. "Let's get the damn books before you have to go night, night!" He growled as he stomped past toward the booth.

Ongie shook his head as he looked over at Will-O. "See, I told you so. He is going to be a bear to deal with for the next month because of this. But then again, Randy is always a big pain in the butt."

"If Randy is as you say, why do you care so much about how he feels about you?" Will-O watched Randy drop then slouch in the booth.

"Randy may be a pain. However, he has been my best friend ever since we could crawl. He is a little conceded, but he is always right by my side when the chips are flying." Ongie slid his arm around Will-O's waist. "Come to think of it; Randy is the cause of most of those chips." He laughed as they followed Randy to the booth.

Will-O Wisp

CHAPTER 8

The bouncer smiled as he allowed the beautiful Mohican woman to lead him off the dance floor. If he read her signals right, he was in for a wild ride tonight. He drew her to him, crushing her tightly against his body. He savored each movement of her body rubbing up against his.

She did not resist his advance. She slid her hand in between their bodies and down the front of his jeans hovering above his crotch and the bulge beneath.

The bouncer quickly drew them behind the pillar at the corner with a large group of potted plants covering the small hidden space behind the column away from the crowd and the ever-watchful eye of the security cameras.

He grabbed her hair, yanking her head back, exposing her luscious plump lips. He crushed his lips against hers, forcing her mouth open as he thrust his tongue deep into her mouth. Much to his surprise and delight, she wrapped her arms around his neck returning the tonsil probe.

Soon, he felt her fingernails digging grooves into his flesh on his back. He broke the lip lock and pried her fingers from his flesh. He held her wrists in one hand as he grabbed the back of her neck, "You came to the right place since you like it rough, I'm your man." He went in for another kiss and found his lip being devoured between her teeth as she purred.

He slapped her in the ear to get her to release his lip. She rubbed her ear with the back of her hand. "Ah, I thought you were a man that likes it rough. You can't even stand a nibble on the lip. I like a man who can take it as much as he can dish it out. White men are all talk and no guts. I'm going back to my high beam walkers. They know how to treat a class act like me."

She turned to leave. His hand clamped down on her upper arm. He yanked her back. His face inches from her. "I do like it rough, and I know just how to treat a classy dame like you. However, we are in my workplace. Come with me and let me clock out then I will show you the wildest night of your Mohican life." He led her out from their hiding place.

He glanced around the casino. The other bouncer was standing over by the entrance. They went over to him. The bouncer nodded towards her, "I have a wild one here. I am escorting her out and making sure she doesn't try to sneak back in." then winked at his co-worker. "Clock me out. I won't be back tonight."

He walked her out of the casino into the employee parking lot when she reached over and clawed his groin. He winced in pain, releasing his hold on her arm as he bent forward trying to pry her hand free of his testicles.

She laughed as she continued through the parking lot dragging the unfortunate man beside her. Each time he tried something to free himself from the excruciating pain, her fingers only dug deeper into his soft flesh.

"Oh my God! Let me go! Stop! I like it rough, but I'm not into B/D. If you want it then for God sake, woman, let go!" the words grounded out through his clenched teeth.

She dragged him up to a blue 2017 McLaren 650S Spider convertible. She released his groin and opened the passenger's car door. She motioned for him to get in as she licked her finger. "Ah come on, I didn't hurt you all that bad. Besides sweet thing, for one night with me, you can have my ride as payment." She caressed the edge of the door. "Just think how many females you can lure to your place with you in the driver's seat."

He tilted his head trying to decide whether to trust her in this deal as he took in what she was offering. The McLaren 650S Spider convertible had all the bells and whistles right down to the seven-speed automatic transmission, leather carbon black bucket seats, diamond art wheel finish, sports exhaust, and Meridian auto surround sound system. He knew he could handle the slim luscious body that she was offering, now that he knew her tricks. "What guarantee do I have that this dream job will be mine after a night of enjoyment hammering you?"

She laughed as she walked around the car and slid into the driver seat. She reached over flipping down the visor and pulled the title out of the sleeve. "Here is the title. To get it, all you have to do is sit your tight buns in the passenger's seat." She waved the title in a come-hither manner.

He slid gently down into the seat and pulled his long legs in then slammed the door shut as he snatched the title. He gave it a quick once-over. The owner's name on the title was M. Wuhti. "What kind of a name is Wuhti?"

She laughed, sliding her seatbelt on before she put the key in the ignition. She started the car, roaring the engine, and then dropped it into reverse, tearing out of the parking space. She shifted it into drive, as she stomped the accelerator, laying him back against the seat. "It's an ancient ancestral name. I've had it for a very long time. Fasten in sweet cheeks; I wouldn't want you to fly out on a tight curve before we arrive at my longhouse."

He snatched the seat belt and struggled to fasten it as she swerved in and out of the aisles then cut off the oncoming traffic as she swung out of the parking lot heading the wrong way on the one-way entrance. She laughed all the louder as car horns blared and tires screamed in protest as drivers swerved out of their way.

Soon she swerved over into the proper lane and headed out of town toward the woods. She smiled as she glanced over watching him grip the door arm, his knuckles turning white from the pressure he was clutching the door arm.

They turned off the main road onto a winding lane. The trees shot past in a blur as she buried the accelerator. She whipped the car around a large tree, through the opening in the wooden wall, slamming on the brakes, kicking up a massive cloud of dust.

When the dust settled, a longhouse came into view, set deep in the compound.

He quickly got out of the car, marveling at the accuracy of what he saw. He walked over to the side of the longhouse. He examined the edge of the longhouse, running his hand over the bark shingles, giving a little whistle. His eyes traveled up the side to the arched roof covered with leaves and grass. Smoke came drifting through the smoke holes.

He turned seeing her leaning against the spider watching him. "Wow! This encampment looks like it could have come straight out of the 1700's. Was this built for the annual Ironwork Festival for a reenactment?" He walked over to the elm-bark canoe, picking up the paddle resting on it. He ran his fingers over the handle worn smooth from years of use.

She laughed as she glided over to him, taking the paddle from him. Her tongue slid over her lips as she leaned down placing the paddle back in its resting place. In doing so, she allowed him a clear view of her ample cleavage. "I have a better idea for your fingers to do than to run over an old paddle." She rose brushing up against him.

She slid her hand into his and led him over to the hide-covered door at the end of the longhouse. As she lifted the latch of the door to go in, he commented on how different the leather looked and asked what animal it was from. She turned her head glancing over her shoulder at him. "It's male."

His brow knitted as they entered the darken longhouse. He could barely make out the low platforms and the shelves above them running the length of the sides of the longhouse. The only lighting was a dwindling fire burning in the fire pit. He slowly walked over to one of the shelves and picked up one of the clay pots sitting on the shelf. He laid it down and picked up an ancient war club. He examined it, finding dark reddish-brown stains on the stone. "If I didn't know better, I would swear this war club was used recently." He gave a low whistle.

"This one is not one of the ones I sent you for." A low growl came from the darken platform across the room behind the fire pit.

"I know Mother. She was guarding them tonight along with a batch of Christian women. I decided he would do as a diversion until she is not with them." She slid the heavy bolt in place, locking the door as a dark thin form crawled off the platform. She smiled drawing his attention from the weak form. "You asked me what kind of hide was covering the door. It is a human male."

He dropped the war club, screaming as Mesa Soyok Wuhti landed on his back, her bloody knife raised high over her head as she grabbed a fist full of his hair, yanking his head back to expose his neck. *"Soyoka-u-u-u!"*

CHAPTER 9

Ongie bade each of the authors good night and told them there would be a VIP pass waiting for them at the front gate of the reservation. Randy did the same and headed back to the casino. Ongie smiled as the women waved goodbye and got into the limo. He looked down at Will-O. "Are you ready to call it a night or would you like to have a chocolate martini with me at the Hard Rock Café and see the falls in the moonlight, waiting for the sun to rise?"

"I never get tired of the falls, and a chocolate martini sounds delightful" Will-O's smile brightened Ongie's soul as he led her to his car.

Soon they were sitting at a small table in the crowded Hard Rock Café. Ongie licked the chocolate off the edge of his martini glass only to have it smear on the side of his mouth. Will-O laughed as she reached over with her napkin to help him out.

Ongie ensnared her hand and drew her to him. He lifted her face to meet his as his lips sought her soft caress of lips on his.

Will-O pulled away from his embrace. Ongie's smile fell at her rebuff. "I'm sorry Willow if I overstepped my bounds. I thought everything was pointing to this."

Will-O took a deep cleansing breath. "It's not that I do not like you Ongie It's just a little too fast. We do not even know each other's full names. I at least want to know a guy's last name before kissing him."

Ongie sat back and smiled. "You are correct on that point. I am sorry I did not properly introduce myself, Willow. My full name is Ongwaterohiathe Whitehorse. Now you can understand why I go by Ongie. Willow is a beautiful name. My tribe uses the willow tree for lots of things."

"My name is not spelled like the tree. It is Will hyphen O. My last name is Wisp. My ancestors came from Scotland centuries ago."

"So, I take it they named you for one of your male ancestors named William."

"No," she laughed. "I am Will-O Wisp. I am named after no ancestor."

"It is delightful to see you smile." Ongie smiled back as he fished in his hip pocket for his wallet. He pulled out a twenty and laid it on the table. He stood and held out his hand to her. "We need to get going if we are going to see the falls at sunrise."

Will-O laughed again, "Okay, the falls are so far away from here, a mere three blocks." as she took his hand.

Ongie smiled as they left. "It may be just three blocks away, but I saunter in the fog."

"Oh, you do, do you?"

"Yes, I do not want to miss any of the sights." He answered as they walked across the street into the park.

They walked along the path watching the fog swirl around them, listening to the roar of the falls. They leaned against the railing watching the colored light show the park was shining on the falls.

The spray from the falls bathed them in a mist. Ongie wrapped his body around Will-O to keep her warm as they watched the sun starting to immerse the Peace Bridge in a golden hue. The rainbow accompanying the rays surpassed anything the light show could offer.

Ongie lightly kissed the top of Will-O's head. "I better get you home, so I can get to the reservation and get the VIP passes ready. Will-O, would you please come and be my guest at the festival. I will be busy, but I will be able to show you around and explain the different activities."

Will-O turned in his arms and hugged him, laying her cheek against his chest. She could hear his steady heartbeat against her ear. She inhaled, breathing in his essence, drawing it deep within her soul before releasing him. "Yes, I will come, but you do not have to take me home. I do not live that far away. I will take a taxi, so you can go get prepared for the festival."

"If that is the way it must be, I will surrender you to a cab. May I give you a small kiss good morning before you go?"

She tilted her head, and Ongie took the initiative drawing her closer, and his lips tenderly met her. An explosion of radiated passion flooded his soul. He drank deeply in the well of her soul pouring out through her lips. The more he drank, the more he craved. It was as if he could not quench the craving the kiss started.

A small giggle registered on his ears as he finally broke the kiss. They glanced over at a group of teenage girls giggling and whispering standing approximately twenty feet from them in the last remaining bits of fog swirling about their feet.

"Well, this is awkward. I never was laughed at for kissing a beautiful woman." Ongie grinned as he took Will-O's hand and led her up to the street to the taxi stand.

…………

The cabbie looked strange as Will-O leaned in the window and told him the address she wanted to go. He started to point out she could walk to it when Will-O put a finger to her lips then turned back to Ongie. She leaned up brushing her lips across his cheek. She opened the door and climbed into the back of the cab.

…………

Ongie slowly closed the door and watched the taxi pull away before he turned to go to his car. The taxicab turned the corner and drove three more blocks and pulled to the curb. Will-O paid the cabbie and turned back to the falls. She strolled through the park, making sure Ongie did not see her. She walked beyond the entrance to the Peace Bridge.

She leaned against the railing watching the river. Will-O glanced around making sure no one could see her before she waved her hand over the river. A ripple formed as a tunnel opening appeared at the edge of the river. Will-O walked into the darkened tunnel. The passageway opening closed in after Will-O. She traveled through the twisting passageway, feeling it shut behind her with every step she took. She turned the corner and walked into the atrium. The Niagara River boiled and churned over the ornate glass dome ceiling. She gave a deep sigh as she picked up the damp cloth from the stand beside the bed. She could still visualize Ongie lying there with the towel over his eyes. She held the fabric to her lips, closing her eyes. A tear slid out down on her cheek.

CHAPTER 10

Preparations were coming to an end for the festival when Jordyn's novel van pulled up to the entrance of the reservation. The group was glad they had chosen to bring the van chuck full of boxes of books on their tour. They had sold half of what they had transported already.

Jordyn rolled down her window as the attendant dressed in full costume came to the door. "Good morning, Ongie Whitehorse has made arrangements for us to come and do readings along with selling our novels."

The attendant looked down his list frowning. He flipped page after page. He shook his head as he looked up at her. "I'm sorry. I do not have you on the list of vendors. I am going to see if I can locate Ongie to see what is going on. They do not always give me the updated list." He pulled out his walkie-talkie and inquired where Ongie was. Soon the walkie-talkie squawked, and a scratchy voice came on telling him Ongie was over at the reenactment village. The voice stated they had a new updated list for him.

"Can you tell me if there is a group of authors on the list and if so where did Ongie place them? Madam, what name would Ongie have put you down under?"

Jordyn smiled and pointed to the side of the van. "Any of the four names you find on the van."

The front covers of novels along with a pair of lust red lips covered the sides of the van.

The walkie-talkie squawked again, "Jordyn Meryl is the name for the group. They are to go to the reenactment village, and Ongie will meet them to show them where to set up."

The attendant gave Jordyn a small map. Jordyn handed the sheet to Sue. "Okay navigator, start directing to the village."

Sue laughed as she looked at the map then at the surrounding area. She pointed to the right. "See those 'I' beam columns standing thirty-five feet in the air? The village is behind them and to the right of them. So, follow this road up the hill, and it should curve around to the village."

"Okay smarty pants, how do you know those are thirty–five-foot columns?" Jordyn put the van in drive and took off following Sue's directions.

"Research my dear, research." LaVina and J.C. laughed at Sue's answer.

They soon arrived at the wooden palisade of the village. Ongie was standing by the gate directing where to place the rest of the artifacts in the settlement. He looked up at the sound of the van's approach and smiled when he saw who it was. He handed the clipboard to a young woman dressed in deerskin. He quickly jogged over to the van. "Hi everyone, I am sorry about the mix-up at the gate. I did set you up with VIP passes, but they must not have reached the gate when you arrived. Let's get you set up; then I will go run down the passes so that you can go to all the events without any problems. We have set you up over by the library and the trading post. May I hitch a ride with you?"

"Sure, hop in the back with LaVina and J.C.. There should be enough room to squeeze you in there somewhere." Jordyn laughed.

Ongie went around to the side door and opened to find LaVina and J.C. sitting in lawn chairs surrounded by boxes full of books, suitcases, table decorations, signs, tent and extra chairs. J.C. had moved several boxes, so Ongie had a small place to sit. He squeezed into the space as he smiled at LaVina. "When you go somewhere you come fully prepared. Wow! You won't need the tent or tables and chairs. We have period tents set up for you."

"We have learned from experience to bring everything under the sun, so we have it if we need it. You do have strong hands to help us unload, correct?" J.C. leaned around a stack of boxes to see Ongie.

"Yes J.C. we have many durable Braves to help the white women with their burdens." Ongie gave a twisted grin as they all burst out laughing. "Jordyn, if you take the next left, that road will take you to the library. The four tents in between the library and trading post are where we set you up. The readings will be over there under that large old willow tree that is coming into view now." He pointed. "We allowed the outer branches to grow to the ground and cut the inner branches to make a lodge-like atmosphere under the tree. In this way, you get the best of both worlds, shade from the hot afternoon sun and still have the breeze to cool you."

Jordyn pulled up in front of the trading post that looked like it came right out of the early 1800's complete with a hitching post for the horses.

Sue got out and opened the side door for the group then reached in and snagged a long bungee cord out of the container. She walked to the front of the van and proceeded to hook one end to the bumper of the van and then wrap the other around the hitching post and hooked it on itself. She turned to see the group staring at her. "What? Haven't you ever seen someone hitch their ride to a post so that it won't wander away? That is what a hitching post is for, you know."

She walked back to the side door and pulled out several boxes loading them up in her arms. They were still standing there looking at her. "What?"

Jordyn shook a finger at her, "One of these days Sue, pow! I'm going to shoot you to the moon!"

Sue laughed as she handed Ongie the boxes and reached in for more. "Naw, I'm not worried. It cost too much for you to do that. Now if you said you were going to blast me with that cannon you carry with you, I would be worried."

CHAPTER 11

Sue walked through the display cases that held artifacts. She was admiring the wampum belts made of beads from shells when an elderly Iroquoian man approached and leaned against the case beside her.

He wore a small three feather Indian cap on the back of his head. His raven black hair was pulled tightly back under the cap then fell to his shoulders. A streak of white hair ran the side of his head. His weathered face had deep crevasses etched in his bronzed skin but could not hide the twinkling deep-set eyes that displayed the merriment of his soul. His outfit was one of the late 1800's. The long shirt was decorated with the same beads as the wampum belts in the case. His leather belt held loops at his sides for a war club and tomahawk. His britches were fringed buckskin. Moccasins completed the outfit.

Sue returned his smile and then turned her attention back to the belts. "These wampum belts are beautiful. They are so detailed. And to think each bead handcrafted from different clam and whelk shells is almost unimaginative."

He glanced at the belts before turning his attention to her. "I see you are a person who indeed appreciates the beauty and hard work that went into crafting a belt."

"Yes, I get so engrossed in the minute details that I lose track of time and usually lose the patience of those with me."

"This is not a typical asset of one who is not a Native American."

Sue placed her hand on the glass case above the largest belt. "My great maternal grandmother said she was half Kickapoo and came to Kansas on the Trail of Tears. She did not realize the Trail of Tears was the Cherokee, Muscogee, Seminole, Chickasaw, Choctaw, and Creek Nations forced march." Sue sighed. "Too bad the only poo she was, smelled. She was a great storyteller though. She also said she was a second cousin of Frank and Jesse James."

"You do not believe her?"

Sue smiled, "Unfortunately, the information we found from genealogical research says she was the second generation American from Scotland in her family. Her grandfather was born in Ross County, Scotland in 1800. You cannot get much more Scot than McCallan. She grew up in Kickapoo, Kansas. That is as close as a Native American as she could have been. It would have been great to listen to her stories."

"So, you never knew her?"

"No, she died when I was little."

"Then how do you know she said these things?"

"Both my mother and my aunt told me about them."

"I see that you found her, Ethiso:da`."

They turned to see Ongie standing behind them.

The elder smiled, "Yes, I have been having a lovely time, and you had to come and interrupt us."

Ongie walked up and placed an arm around his shoulder. "Sue, I would like to introduce you to my Ethiso:da`. Most people know him by Goyathlay Whitehorse." He smiled. "Ethiso:da`, this is the exceptionally talented author, Sue Raymond."

Sue put out her hand, "It is a pleasure to meet you Mr. Whitehorse. I take it that Ethiso:da` means Grandfather."

"It means 'our grandfather.' He is forever claiming any and all children that will accept him. The games are starting. You won't want to miss Ethiso:da` doing the column climb. He is one of the oldest ironworkers that are still on the job." Ongie smiled with pride.

Goyathlay patted Ongie on the back. "Yes, I am, and I can still outclimb you any day of the week."

"That's because you are half-monkey. Clan Mother wishes to have a few words with you before it's your turn to climb the column. You know how she gets if you ignore her."

"Yes, yes, she always wants a few words with me. She will keep, Ongie. I am going to escort Otetiani to the games." Goyathlay held his arm out to Sue.

Sue smiled as she wrapped her hand around the crook of his arm. Goyathlay returned the smile. "Make way Ongie; we would not want to keep Clan Mother waiting."

Ongie stepped back by the kachina dolls as Goyathlay escorted Sue by him. "Ethiso:da`, you do know Otetiani means HE is prepared, not she?"

"In this case Ongie, I include it to mean she. For Ms. Raymond is organized in her information on the Iroquois Nation as I am sure she is in their customs. Now stop bothering me and go about your duties to make sure everything is perfect for our guests. Clan Mother will not be pleased with you if you fail in making this the greatest event of the year."

CHAPTER 12

She stood in the shadows watching the crowd weave through the exhibits and the Iron Workers events for her quarry. Mesa Soyok Wuhti was not pleased they escaped last night. The bouncer only made her craving for their heads in her cauldron acute.

Mesa had followed Goyathlay Whitehorse back from the Hopi nation many years ago. Here she found lush lands filled with naïve children who thought she was only a myth, something to frighten them around the campfire at night. The Katsinas would come at her call if she needed them. The ogres were her protection from those who would stop her from stealing those she chose.

For now, the only ones who opposed her were Goyathlay and the wisp. Goyathlay tried to educate those he loved, his stories. These attempts did not bother her. In fact, they implanted a connection with their unconscious that allowed her access to them as they slept.

The wisp was another matter. She had the power to stop Mesa, but Mesa's skills were growing stronger every year.

Goyathlay barely escaped Mesa Soyok Wuhti many years ago. He still wears the scar across his neck today that her knife made in the dead of night. The wisp was able to deflect the blade enough to prevent his death. The authorities wrote it off as the consequence of a drunken brawl. Goyathlay headed home as soon as he got out of the hospital. The Wisp was always in the shadow alert for a pending attack the whole way back to Niagara.

Her daughter appeared next to her, dressed in a white doeskin dress decorated with purple quahog clam beads sprinkled with white channeled whelk beads. High white doeskin boots covered her shapely legs. "Mother, I still do not understand why I must wear these ridiculous shapeless things. Allow me to wear something that is more form-fitting, and I will be able to obtain you all the heads you would ever want for your cauldron."

Mesa turned, "Obstinate cur! If I wished everyone to know we were here, I would throw you out in the middle of the hoop dancers butt naked. I can feel the wisp is here somewhere lurking in the shadows. The four Christian writers strengthen her powers. Their faith adds to her ability to ward off any attack I would try. Dressed this way, you have a chance to reach our quarry without drawing the wisp's attention."

"And which one of delicious hunks do you want first?" She licked her lips in anticipation.

Mesa Soyok Wuhti pointed the bloody knife at the broad back strapping on climbing equipment. "That one, the one they call Naulowa."

"Yummy, please allow me to play with our food before you gut him like a trout."

"Granted." Mesa shimmered as she disappeared.

Will-O Wisp

CHAPTER 13

Randy turned as Goyathlay left Sue at the edge of the arena and trotted over to the equipment. "Well, it is about time, old man. I thought you were going to forgo the column climb for a less strenuous event like watermelon eating."

Goyathlay picked up his equipment and inspected it before he buckled it on and changed his shoes. He then turned to Randy and smiled. "Randy, you missed the first round of the packing competition. They disqualified you. Maybe you should try entering contests more to your diminished abilities instead of trying to compete with adult men."

Randy's cheeks puffed in and out as he sought to maintain his composure. His eyes narrowed as he yanked his gloves on.

Goyathlay chuckled as he made sure all his equipment was adequately secure then went over to the nearest column. "Well, are you going to try and beat me or go play with the papooses?"

Randy's brow knitted and drew down almost covering his eyes as he walked over to the other beam. He shook his arms to limber up. The starter called out, "Get ready!" Both men took their stance at the column. "Get set!" They grabbed the column with their gloved hands. "Go!"

Randy sprinted up toward the top of the column and the coveted bell. He reached halfway when he heard Goyathlay's bell ring loud and clear then Goyathlay chuckling as he started his track back down the column. Randy gritted his teeth as he finished his climb and rung the bell.

They were posting the times when he made it back down the column. Goyathlay's time: fifty-five seconds. Randy was able to make it in one minute forty-three seconds, still well within the three-minute time frame to place for points. His mouth twitched in frustration as he removed his equipment. He laid the gear down and stormed off through the crowd.

He stomped to the beer tent. Randy slapped his hand down on the bar to gain the bartender's attention. The bartender shook his head and pulled a large can of beer from the cooler then came over and set it down on the bar in front of Randy.

Randy popped the tab on the can then guzzled it down and slammed it on the bar. The bartender retrieved another beer and gave it to Randy. Randy groaned as he held the cold can against his head.

"I take it from your reaction you went up against Goyathlay on the column and lost to the old mountain goat again."

Randy shook his head, "How in the hell can he still be so agile after so many years? He even beat his best time last year."

A soft hand slipped up and took the can of beer. Randy followed his beer to see who pilfered it. The beautiful woman from the casino filled his vision. A broad smile spread across his face wiping away any trace of the scowl that was there moments ago.

She pursed her luscious lips against the side of the can before she snapped the top open and poured her mouth full. She grabbed Randy placing him in a lip lock. She forced the beer into his mouth as his lips parted.

Randy was so surprised that he choked on the beer as it hit the back of his throat. She laughed as he tried to clear his throat. When he stopped coughing, he found her probing tongue where the beer was seconds ago. Her hands wrapped around his body exploring every tiny nook and cranny as they went.

Randy wrapped his arms around her, drawing her in against his rapidly hardening body. The longer he kissed her; the more his body craved her touch. Her essence filled the recesses of his soul which yearned for more.

Randy gasped for air when she finally allowed him to come up for air. He ran his finger across her lips and found it captured with a vice-like suction of her mouth. He pulled his finger halfway out only to feel it deeper embedded in her throat as she inhaled.

Her hand found his belt and started unbuckling it. Randy quickly snagged her hand, pulling it behind him and away from depantsing him. "Oh Baby, where did you go last night? I looked everywhere for you."

She released his finger with a pop. She finished off his beer. A smile spread across her lips. "Oh, sweet thing, I just couldn't wait for you, but I am here now and am all yours for as long as you can stand it."

Randy ground his body against hers as he drank from the well of desire again. This time it was she that gasped for air when they parted.

The bartender rapped Randy on the shoulder. "Hey, you need to take this to a more private place. Clan Mother would have my hide if I allow you to turn this tent into an orgy palace."

Randy grinned as he loosened his hold on her. "Sure, I wouldn't want to give old Ongie a black eye in Clan Mother's eyes because he could not keep everyone in line during this festival."

She grabbed his hand and led him out of the tent. "Quick come with me. I know of a private place that no one will bother us. We can explore each other to our heart's content."

Randy slid his arm around her waist. "Oh Baby, lead on! I am more than ready for you."

She laughed as she led him through the crowd toward the wooden palisade of the village. She diverted her path as they came close to the four tents between the trading post and the museum. She led him down the alley behind the other buildings and toward the back of the palisade. Once there, she drew Randy to her for another tonsillectomy before she squeezed through a small gap in the fence.

Randy had a more difficult time squeezing his bulk through the small opening. Both skin and cloth were left behind by the time he made it through.

She gently blew across the raw skin. The pains cooled and eased as a stronger desire replaced the pain. Randy wrapped his arms around her, drawing her hungrily to his yearning lips. She slid her hand up and pushed him away from her. "Not here, I have a better place. You can scream your head off, and no one will be able to hear you." She called over her shoulder as she ran into the woods.

"It's not going to be me screaming by the time this ends!" Randy ran after the luscious fleeing body disappearing through the trees.

Randy lost her several times in the trees when he would stop to take a breath. The woods were getting denser, and the small path they were on was becoming non-existent. The white doeskin dress flashed among the leaves giving Randy glimpses of hope he would catch her soon ending this game of 'catch me if you can.'

He rounded a large tree trunk to find one of her boots lying on the ground. He picked it up and slid it under his belt. Randy wiped the sweat from his mouth with the back of his hand as he searched for where she went.

He found a purple quahog clam bead under the edge of a bush and another a few feet away on a deer path running back into the undergrowth. He followed the footpath as it wound through the brush and briers. Randy cursed as a brier ripped through his shirt and scratched his stomach. Anger was starting to replace the desire that had burnt blistering moments before.

Randy pushed through the rest of the briers to find himself at the edge of a small stream. He stood on the pebbled shoreline with his hands on his hips, glancing around. Randy shook his head in disbelief. None of this part of the woods looked familiar. He could not believe that she had got him lost. He and Ongie traipsed through the woods surrounding the reservation all their lives. There was no part of the woods unfamiliar to him. Randy was at a loss on how to explain where he was.

He spied a small moccasin imprint at the edge of the water. She had passed this way not long ago. There were small rocks that made a winding path across the stream near the imprint and on the other side of the creek laid the other white boot.

Randy smiled as he started across the creek. His foot slipped on a moss-covered rock, and he found himself sitting in the middle of the stream up to his chest. Randy shook his head and started to rise when the stream bed sucked his foot down in the mire. Randy reached over and grabbed the rock for support as he tried to lift his foot. The stone came free, and Randy found both of his feet sinking rapidly in the mire. He clawed at anything within reach to help him, but it only made the suction that much stronger and sank up to his neck in the water.

Panic struck, and Randy started floundering, his arms splashing the water everywhere. He stretched his neck as high as he could to try to keep his head above the water. He heard laughter then she appeared standing at his head leaning over him.

She placed her hands on her knees, "What on earth are you doing? The stream is not deep enough to do the backstroke."

"Help Me! I'm stuck in quicksand!" Randy spat water out that flowed in as he tried to speak.

She burst into a full body laugh as she shoved his head under the water. Randy's face hit the pebbled bottom of the stream. Shock ran through his body as he realized he was lying upon the pebbled base and no longer stuck in quicksand.

He turned over and pushed himself free of the water. He stood there staring at her sitting there under the tree still laughing at him. Randy's face turned crimson as he sloshed out of the stream to stand in front of her.

"What in the hell just happened? One second I was stuck up to my neck in the mire, and the next second there was a pebbled streambed under me. Where in the hell are we? I know every inch of the woods around the reservation, and you can't tell me we're in those woods. So how did we wind up here?"

She laughed and swung her head allowing her hair to rotate in an arc around her as she picked up her boot from the shore. She threw the thigh boot at Randy's face as she disappeared around the tree. "Catch me before I'm completely nude and you may have the pleasure of completing the removal and have your wildest sex dreams fulfilled."

Randy grabbed the wet boot as the fringe slapped him in the face. He tucked it with the other as he took off after her. He had a hard time keeping her in sight as his mind continued bringing vivid visions of what he wanted to do once he caught her.

He found her headband hanging on a bush as he flew by. He lost her in the dense underbrush. Randy started cursing under his breath as he pressed through the small path in the brushwood. He broke free of the brush and ran into an ancient wooden palisade.

Her bare footprints in the mud ran along the palisade. Randy followed as fast as he could, slipping every few feet in the muck. His hands were raw and full of splinters by the time he reached the palisade's opening. Her doeskin dress lay in the mud against the pole.

Randy picked it up, breathing in her essences lingering on it. He hung the dress on his arm as he marveled at the accuracy of what he saw. He walked over to the dugout then started over to the longhouse when, swoosh, he found himself swinging upside down from a snare in the tree.

As he sway to, and fro, the gate slammed shut on the palisade. She stood there naked watching him hang down by his ankle. She sauntered over and smiled at his plight. "You did not achieve catching me before I was naked. However, I have caught you fully clothed. So that makes me the victor in our challenge. I get to have my wildest dreams with you."

Randy smiled at that. She twirled him as fast as she could. The rope twisted upon itself raising Randy higher and higher. Randy finally had the foresight to throw his arms out to try and slow the spin. Everything was becoming a blur. It looked as if she was growing taller and deforming.

Randy shut his eyes trying to keep his equilibrium. He opened them when the rope finally stopped its upward climb. There standing before him no longer was a beautiful naked woman but a Katsina. The ogre reached up with a hairy paw halted the rope from unwinding. It leaned in, its face just inches from Randy's. It's reeking breath gagged Randy.

"Why are you gagging sweet thing? You weren't gagging when I was French kissing you in the beer tent. You were asking for so much more." Its warty tongue slithered out of slime-covered lips and slid up the side of Randy's face.

Randy fought to get away from the foul creature. His face froze in terror. The Katsina laughed as it released the rope and Randy started his downward spiral into terror. His screams echoed through the woods.

Will-O Wisp

CHAPTER 14

Goyathlay slid his arms around an elderly lady dressed in a ceremonial costume covered in clam and whelk shells. He gave her a small peck on the cheek before releasing her.

She shook her finger at him as Goyathlay captured it kissing it as she pulled her finger free. She drew her brow down as she drew a deep breath, "Old Man, I sent for you over a half an hour ago. I know you received my message. When will you stop ignoring me? I wanted you to be by my side at the opening ceremony." She shook her head. "You're late as usual."

Goyathlay only smiled as he drew her to him. "I was being impressed by one of the authors Ongie invited to join us today."

"I know you. Your head turns whenever there is a female within a mile of you." She smiled back at him. "Now introduce me to our guest."

Ongie jogged up and gave the elderly lady a warm embrace as he kissed the top of her head. She gave him a stern frown in response. However, the twinkle emitting from her brown eyes told another story. "See Grandmother; I told you I would find and rein him in for your chastisement." He turned to Sue. "Grandmother, I would like to introduce you to one of our special guests, Author Sue Raymond. Sue, this is our tribe's clan mother, Aarushi Whitehorse, who also is my pleasure to have as my maternal grandmother."

Sue put her hand out in greeting, "It's a pleasure to meet you, ma'am. I want to thank you for allowing my friends and me to be part of all this."

A wisp of a smile set on her face as she shook Sue's hand. "You are welcome to be our guest of the clan on this day. We are thankful Ongie had the foresight to invite you to be our guest. Ongie has informed me of your group's generous donation to our library. For this, our tribe thanks you from the bottom of our hearts."

Sue's cheeks redden, "You are most welcome. It was our pleasure to help the library." Her wristwatch alarm sounded. She shut it off. "Forgive me for having to leave. That was my five-minute warning to get prepared for my turn to do a reading. I hope you might have a few minutes to spare to hear it. I will be reading one of my children books, *'Grampa's House Needs Painting.'*"

Aarushi nodded, "I will try." She turned to Goyathlay. "Come, old man, I have need of you. Ongie, you take care of our guests while I attend to what I must." She crossed her arms and slowly walked away, making sure Goyathlay was following.

Will-O Wisp

CHAPTER 15

They traveled in silence through the throng as children ran back and forth through the crowd trying to beat the other to the next event. The kids shoved corn dogs in their mouths as they went. The two climbed the wooden staircase attached to the side of the general store to the small office over the shop.

Goyathlay opened the door allowing Aarushi to enter first before following her, closing the door behind them.

She turned, her face shadowed with concern. Goyathlay laid a hand on her shoulder. She brushed it off. "She is here."

Goyathlay drew back at her rebuff. "What female are you talking about, old woman? There are thousands of women mulling around today."

Aarushi huffed as her brows drew down into a scowl. "I said nothing about a woman. I said SHE is back."

Goyathlay's lips twisted, "You are talking loco. If she is not a woman what is she?"

Aarushi ran her finger along the scar on his neck. "The one who gave you this."

He grabbed her hand and held it firm. "You are sure of this? You have seen her?"

"No, but I have felt the evil she emits. It is crawling around our young seeking to devour those not under the Lord's protection."

Goyathlay drew her trembling body into his strong embrace. "We have defeated her before; we can do it again."

Aarushi shuddered, "This time she is not alone. She has brought one just as evil with her. I fear there will be much death; many heads will fill her basket if the wisp cannot stop her. I have prayed the Lord would again send us the wisp's protection. However, the answer has not come. For I do not feel the wisp's presence, only evil crawling over my soul."

Goyathlay stiffed, "It all makes sense now. Old Crow said Ongie jumped into the river to rescue a woman that fell. He was mumbling through his beer that he tried to stop Ongie by screaming she was not real. We all thought it was the beer talking as usual.

Aarushi we must warn Ongie!" He turned toward the door.

"No, he will only think we have been in your firewater and pay us no more mind than he did Old Crow. Your stories of Mesa Soyok Wuhti has made her no more than a fairy tale to our youth. Mesa Soyok Wuhti in their mind is in the same category as the Easter Bunny and Santa Claus. Do not give me that scowl. I know you intended to educate them about the dangers lurking in the dark. Unfortunately, they live in a world that monsters only live in the movies." She flipped her hand waving him off.

"Since the wisp has not come to answer your prayers then I will warn the False Face Society of the danger to the clan. Maybe together we can ward off Mesa until the wisp comes to our rescue. I have to go now so I can change up the lineup in the show." He gave her a firm hug before he left the office.

Aarushi stood there with her eyes closed as she tried to gain her composure before she returned to her duties as Clan Mother.

CHAPTER 16

Ongie came into the beer tent and went up to the bar. The bartender nodded to Ongie as he served two beers to a guy with a gal hanging on his back. The bartender wiped the counter before he made his way over to Ongie. He handed Ongie a beer before starting to make his intentions known to the woman in the tight fitting jeans and tank top barely covering her ripe breasts. She flipped her cowboy hat down across her eyes as her eyes fluttered come hither.

Ongie snagged the bartender by the arm before he got away. "Hey, have you seen Randy around? He was supposed to be overseeing the kids' games. No one I've talked to has seen him since the beam climb."

"If the gal he was with earlier today has anything to say about it, Randy won't be surfacing anytime soon. I had to remind them this was only a beer tent and not a brothel. She had almost depanted him before I was able to pull them apart long enough to put the fear of Clan Mother in Randy's lust soaked brain. She led him away like a lamb to the slaughter."

Ongie shook his head in disgust as he took a swig from the bottle then slammed it on the counter so hard it broke sending beer and shards of glass across the bar. "When will he grow up enough to not allow his lust to control his reasoning? Sorry about the mess. Did you see which way they went?"

The bartender grabbed a bar towel to clean up the mess. "They went out the back of the tent an hour ago more or less. I doubt you will find them until she finishes with him."

Ongie pulled money out of his pocket laying it on the counter for beer. "Have you seen this woman before?"

The bartender shook his head, "No. I would have remembered that booty if I saw it before. I wish she would have paid me half the attention she was lavishing on Randy." He waved his hand over an imaginary female figure.

Ongie drew a deep breath to try to calm the aggravation growing in the pit of his stomach before leaving out the back of the tent. He was able to pick up Randy's tracks because of the symbol Randy cut into the heel of his boot. The trail soon led Ongie to the hole in the palisade, and the small amount of blood Randy left behind when he squeezed through.

Ongie was sizing up the hole to see if he could wedge through without tearing something or allowing something to gouge him when his walkie-talkie went off. He grumbled to himself that Randy would have to wait as he turned back to the job at hand.

Goyathlay was standing on the stage with the False Face Society behind him in a semi-circle, each had a drum in one hand, and an animal hide shaker decorated with eagle feathers when Ongie got to the grand stage. This configuration was one they used during a healing ceremony.

Ongie flipped through the schedule on the clipboard. Goyathlay was not scheduled. What was he up to? Ongie started to the stage to stop his grandfather who by the looks of things was about to embark upon one of his very long stories. A hand took him by the elbow halting his advance. Ongie glanced down into his grandmother's eyes.

"No Ongie, do not try to stop your grandfather. He has my permission to alter the schedule. Stay and listen well, Ongie. This story is as much for you as it is for all the youth in the audience."

Goyathlay nodded his head in a slow rhythm. The rest of the Society picked up the beat. The drums and shakers tapped the background music as Goyathlay now swayed to the tune of the drums. He started humming as he step-danced to the rhythm. The pace picked up speed until Goyathlay was bouncing from one end of the stage to the other. The dance went on for several minutes until he was at center stage. Suddenly, Goyathlay's hands stretched to the Heavens, his feet landed with a solid thud, stopping everything, drawing everyone's attention to him.

"Good day, on behalf of the Wolf Clan of the Iroquois Nation, we greet you all to our first combined PowWow and Iron Workers Festival. I am Goyathlay, leader of the False Face Society, and meek husband to our tribe's Clan Mother Aarushi Whitehorse." This brought a loud, full body laugh from the crowd plus a few rebuffs on Goyathlay's meekness.

He gave a broad smile before continuing, "Ah, I see my fantastic reputation proceed me with quite a few of you in the crowd. We have changed the schedule slightly to bring you a message of great urgency. Clan Mother who is also our spiritual leader has detected a great evil is walking among us. This maliciousness is coming in the form of Mesa Soyok Wuhti. For those who have not had the opportunity of being at one of my campfires, I will tell you all about Mesa Soyok Wuhti. The name translates into 'Monster Woman.'

"This evil followed me back from the Hopi Nation when I was too ignorant to pay attention to the warning of my elders. It was late in the evening when I first encountered Mesa Soyok Wuhti. I was traveling alone between villages. The elders warned me not to walk alone at night. However, I was a young robust brave back then. Nothing scared me. About halfway through my journey, going through a rocky gorge, I heard a slight scraping sound on rocks up behind me and to the right.

"I slowed my steps so I could distinguish what made the sound. They told me a family of mountain lions prowled this part of the gorge. I unstrapped the thong over my knife realizing how foolish my actions had become. One Bowey knife against two and a half inch razor sharp claws did not make good odds for my survival.

"I did not believe a lion made this sound. Their claws stay sheathed in their paws until they pounce on their prey. This sound was metallic against a stone. When I stopped, the noise ceased. It mimicked my steps. This went on for about a half a mile as the scrapping came closer and louder.

"By the time I finally got up the courage to confront whatever was following me the scraping became unbearable. My heart hammered in my chest with my breath coming in spurts. I withdrew my knife, my knees slightly bent as I balanced on the ball of my feet in anticipation. I drew a breath as I screamed, 'Come and face me, coward, for I tire of this stupid game of cat and mouse.' Then I waited.

"My eyes darted from dark shadow to the next trying to distinguish who or what made the sounds. Then I saw it in between the large boulders, crawling in the shadows. I could not make out what it was but knew this was the source of the scrapping. Somehow it had managed to get in front of me and was hiding in the shadows waiting to take me unaware. I tensed in anticipation of the attack.

"Slowly it crawled toward me, staying in the thick shadows. The moon appeared from behind a cloud shining a moonbeam into the darkness revealing a small, slim figure. Its long scraggly hair fell in front of its face. The bony frame looked too frail even to hold up the grimy torn deerskin that hung on it. The knife drug along the side of the boulder. It sent sparks from the blade. It came closer. It lifted its head revealing deep-set black eyes over thin lips. The lips parted as jagged fang teeth slid over them. Its mouth twisted into a snarl as its arm came up in a jerky movement holding the knife over its head in an arc.

"It cackled, 'Soyoka-u-u-u,' it rose before me. The knife aimed at my heart as it sprang lightning fast. I deflected the knife with my blade inches from my chest. It's long fingernails dug into the flesh of the back of my hand as it tried to claw my blade free from my grip.

"I backhanded it with my left fist knocking it away from me but in doing so lost my balance. I fell on my side, pinning my knife beneath me. It pounced again as I landed, clawing at my eyes as the blade dug deep in my left forearm. I flipped on my back trying to dislodge it as I freed my knife. The hand flew from my eyes to my blade, ripping it from my grasp. My knife landed at least fifteen feet out of my reach. I swung my leg up and around its chest as it drew back to plunge the knife into my chest. I straighten my leg throwing it away from me.

"It rolled away, coming up in a crouch ready for another round as the cackle 'Soyoka-u-u-u' filled my soul with dread. I was able to gain my footing in time to do a rolling throw as it sprang. Both of my forearms were bleeding profusely as the knife slashed and hacked. I fell over a rock as I felt the blade enter the skin of my throat." Goyathlay stopped, glaring out at the audience. "So you do not believe me! Then take a good long look at the truth!" He grabbed the beaded necklace surrounding his throat and yanked it free.

Beads fell, bouncing across the stage as the stunned audience stared at the sizeable jagged scar running across Goyathlay's throat. Ongie stood staring at his grandfather's revelation. He had heard different versions of this story over the years growing up at the campfire but never had the story rung with so much truth as now. Goyathlay's beaded necklace had always been a part of his attire as long as Ongie could remember. Aarushi made it for Goyathlay when he came back from New Mexico before they were married.

Goyathlay allowed the rest of the necklace fall to the stage as he stomped off. The crowd parted at his approach. Aarushi threaded her way after him as the False Face Society started a dance to break the tension in the group.

. . . .

Aarushi found Goyathlay in the museum leaning against the war club display case. She laid her hand on his shoulder. He gave a deep sigh shrugging his shoulders.

"Old woman, they did not believe me, even with the proof staring them in the face. How much more can I do to make them believe?"

"As the Bible states, they have ears but cannot hear, they have eyes but cannot see. So many choose to disregard what they cannot explain away no matter how many warnings were given of the coming disaster. It took Noah a hundred years to build the ark, and in the end, only eight people obeyed and climbed into the ark before the Lord shut the door, allowing the rest of the citizens to drown because of their sins. We can only do what we can along with prayer for the Lord's protection and guidance. Do not beat yourself up. Each must accept the Lord's salvation and protection through Christ Jesus. No one can do it for them. We pray, teach, and live in a way that glorifies the Lord so they can see and want that. Come, we will go to my office and pray for our nation and their protection against this latest attack from evil."

. . . .

Ongie made sure things were going smoothly on the stage before he turned his thoughts back to Randy's disappearance. He wondered if Randy was worth the effort to go hunt him up or just do it himself. "No. I'm not covering for him again. Randy said he would do it, so it's time I hold him accountable to his word." Ongie said aloud a bit too loud as he stomped off. The crowd parted getting out of his way.

Ongie's anger cooled off by the time he reached the willow tree. There standing at the edge of the branches was the girl of his dreams. Will-O's dress was white chiffon with a billowy skirt that had black trees and birds silhouettes on it. Seeing Will-O, drained the rest of anger lingering in his soul. He walked up behind her, sliding his arms around her waist, drawing her to him as he leaned down, kissing the hollow of her neck.

"I'm so glad you decided to attend. I need some distraction."

"So Mr. Whitehorse, I am just a distraction for you? What distraction do your thoughts need to be distracted from? You look very handsome this afternoon in your leather vest and beaded chest piece." She slid her hand over the wolf tattoo on his right triceps. "Not wearing a shirt gets everyone the opportunity to see your tribal tattoo."

Ongie smiled, "Thank you, not very many people understand the meaning of my tattoo. How is it that you would know such things, not being a Native American?"

Will-O smiled as she leaned her head on his chest. "I have known about tribal tattoo since Celtic times."

Ongie raised her head with a finger under the chin. "What was that? You spoke too softly."

"I was just stating tribal tattooing traditions span many different cultures over centuries. Say, where were you headed before you saw me? You told me you needed to be distracted."

Ongie released her, then took her hand as he ignored her question. He turned his attention to J.C. reading from her latest novel a few minutes before starting to walk on. At the corner of the general store, Ongie stopped and drew a deep breath. "Well, I need to go find Randy. He took off with some girl for a bit of fun, and no one has seen him since. This time I'm not going to allow him to get away with shucking his responsibility. Please stick around. It shouldn't take me too long to run him down and pull him back on track. Then we can spend some time together on my lunch hour."

Will-O gave Ongie a weak smile as he released her hand and walked toward the back of the building. Will-O bowed her head as she listened to the wind blowing through the leaves. She nodded in agreement to the whisper in the wind. She felt a soft hand on her shoulder. Will-O looked up at the concerned face of LaVina.

"I don't mean to intrude but is everything alright? You seem slightly worried."

"Thank you for your concern. I have a huge favor to ask your group of authors."

"Sure, what can we help you with?"

"Please gather together someplace out of the way and form a prayer circle for protection for Ongie and Randy. Randy is in danger, and Ongie has gone looking for him."

"Shouldn't we call the authorities for help if they are in trouble?"

"No. The authorities would not be able to assist them. Your prayers are what they need the most. Forgive me, but I must be on my way." Will-O turned and dashed down the path after Ongie.

CHAPTER 17

Ongie had to force one of the boards loose in the palisade to be able to squeeze through the opening. Once through, he looked around for a trace of where Randy went. Ongie was glad for all the tracking excursions Goyathlay drug him on when they were young. Of the two boys, Ongie was the best tracker. Randy could never locate him when it was Randy's turn to track Ongie, where Ongie always was able to find Randy within fifteen minutes of the game. The only one Ongie could not locate was Goyathlay. It seemed like they could look for hours with no luck, then when they gave up and plopped down under a tree to rest, then they would hear Goyathlay laughing at them in the very branches of the tree they were sitting under. Many times, they had even climbed the same tree looking for him and missed seeing the elusive old man.

Ongie started along the palisade trailing the path Randy left. Soon the trail took Ongie down a small deer path. The forest closed in around Ongie in dark shadows. The shadows tried to blot out the trail. He kept to the footpath, catching a glimpse of Randy's heel print in the dirt between the fallen leaves. The trees thinned out into thickets eager to take their place.

Ongie stopped to take a breath before venturing into the mass of thickets. The air had gone hot and stale, creating a perception of something ancient. He glanced around trying to get his bearings. This part of the forest seemed unfamiliar and forbade. A film of sweat coated his body making his clothes cling to him like a scratchy second skin. Ongie thought of leaving his quarry to whatever fate was waiting for Randy in comparing the pain he would endure traveling through the thicket path if you could call it a pathway.

Ongie pulled his handkerchief from his hip pocket wiping the stinging sweat out of his eyes. It became drenched in sweat. He rung it out the best he could then took opposing corners and twirling it into a band for his forehead in an attempt to keep the sweat out of his eyes.

Once done, Ongie started weaving his way through the thickets. He wished he had more on than just his vest to protect his skin from the brier branches. The thorns pierced his skin on his hands and arms leaving thin bloody trails in their wake. Soon Ongie was leaving a trail of his own, one of blood.

He broke free of the thickets at the edge of a stream. Ongie knelt cleansing the wounds in the clear water. He kept a wary eye on the surrounding area wondering where he was. He had never come across this part of the forest nor this stream. The stream soon had a trace of pink from the bloody wounds. It washed the trail quickly downstream along with the scent of fresh blood with it.

....

The Katsina lifted its head. Its enormous nostrils drew in the breeze and the scent on it. The smell excited the beast. There was new prey in the forest.

"Mother! Can you smell it? Fresh quarry has entered our domain on his own."

"This one is different from the one in the cage. This one is strong in courage. But along with the bravery, is foolishness in his faithfulness to his friends."

"You are correct, Mother. Only a fool would dare follow me into our forest. The thickets have done their job well. The scent of blood is pungent. I will have no trouble tracking this one down. Please allow me the pleasure of hunting our prey down. This one was way too easy to catch." She swung the cage to and fro.

"Go and collect our new prize while I get his accommodations ready for his arrival." Mesa grabbed the ogre by the arm. "Make sure you don't sample the merchandise before I am ready for him."The monster pulled free with a silent snarl on its lips. The door slammed shut in its wake.

Randy laid whimpering on the bottom of the cage. Mesa drew near the swinging cage. Her foul breath gagged Randy's whimpers into submission. She grabbed the enclosure halting the swing. Randy slammed into the bars his arms splayed to minimize the pain coursing through his body.

....

Ongie started across the stream. What had been only ankle deep swiftly became waist high, pulling to dislodge his footing with every step. Ongie became aware of a low growl as he approached the middle of the stream. Ongie glanced around as he slowly reached for his knife at his waist. The noise became louder as he slid the knife out of the sheath. Ongie raised the blade in a defensive position as the direction of the growling. It was now in front of him in the underbrush. A howl drowned out all sound as the ogre broke free of the brush, charging Ongie.

Ongie raised his knife to meet the attack. The ogre was ten feet from him when something struck Ongie in the back driving him under the water. As his face hit the bottom of the stream, he fell through the bed into a damp tunnel. The opening closed behind him, entombing him in darkness. He landed with a resounding thud. The knife flew from his hand.

Ongie hacked the water out of his lungs as he drew his hands and feet under him. He slowly rose to his feet feeling around to familiarize himself with the surroundings. The tunnel was large enough for Ongie to stand erect. Its width was approximately five to six feet. Ongie reach overhead to see if he could locate the trap door he fell through. The only thing he felt was dirt and tree roots. He felt behind him finding another earthen wall blocking the way.

Ongie felt with his foot in front of him as he walked to make sure he was not stepping into another abyss, waving his arms to prevent any low-hanging obstacles. His eyes strained to find any fragment of light in the total darkness. They sent shards of red and blue reminiscence of shadows of lumination on his retinas from the light seconds before he fell. Each step Ongie took seemed like an eternity.

Wham! The dirt wall hit Ongie in the back. Terror gripped him as the wall pushed Ongie forward while the sides closed against his hands. His mind screamed, if he did not get out of the tunnel, he would be buried alive. Ongie ran for his life. The shaft grew tighter with every step slapping the floor. Ongie bent over clawing at the walls to make it through the tiny opening. He stumbled forward falling face first onto a quartz floor. The tunnel closed behind him.

Ongie rolled over on his back. His chest throbbed trying to draw air into his burning lungs. His mind refused to believe what his eyes saw. Overhead the Niagara river boiled being held back by a glass dome.

. . . .

Mesa slid the knife across the bars of the cage. Each click of the blade sent shards of terror racing through Randy's nerves making his body convulse with tremors. Her lips slid back exposing sharp bloodstained fangs. "Excellent, your fear permeates the atmosphere of the lodge." She drew a deep breath then her tongue slid over the fangs as if she was tasting the fear. "Soon, very soon I will sample your flesh as I flay it from the bones, filling my kettle full. Winter is coming, and I must prepare my larder for the long winter nights. I have done this for centuries so I have honed my skills and you will last for months. Once you are used up, I will start in on your friend, Ongie Whitehorse. I hope he tastes as good as his grandfather. Too bad I only got a tiny sample of his flesh."

Randy's screams of No mingled with her cackling. Mesa turned away and tugged the black kettle from the lower shelf then hung it on the iron tripod over the firepit.

....

The ogre roared in rage as it tore at the stream bed trying to reach Ongie. Soon the stream was filled with the stench from the rocks tearing gashes in its fingers. A twig snapped behind it. The ogre whirled around spying Will-O on the bank. Will-O dressed in legging and a leather vest now. The fiend's face drew into a tight snarl. A loud bellow erupted from it as it charged, claws extended posed to tear Will-O's throat out. Water sprayed everywhere from the wide feet landing on the edge of the stream, in a crouch, ready to spring on Will-O.

Will-O stood patiently waiting for the charging ogre. The monster launched, claws and fangs ready to tear Will-O's heart out. It landed with a thud. Will-O now stood behind the prostrated ogre. The beast twisted up on one knee, facing Will-O. Foam ran out of the corner of its mouth as it jumped at Will-O. It landed face first in the stream.

The ogre grabbed a fist full of rocks and mud slinging it at Will-O, only to find her not there. The rocks landed harmlessly on the shore. It roared in frustration. It raised its shaggy head. The hair slid from its face as it howled. The ogre drew its legs under it as it sized up the situation. It calculated its next move and launched its attack sideways, only to land up against the nearest tree in the grove. A smile crossed Will-O's lips at the fiend's miscalculation.

The monster grabbed a sapling by the trunk and ripped it from the ground roots and all. It charged Will-O, swinging the sapling like a club. Will-O stood her ground dodging it with ease. The ogre brought the tree high overhead, bringing it down in a flash to cleave Will-O in two.

Will-O caught the sapling one-handed during midswing. It sent a jarring wave of pain through the ogre. Will-O ripped it free from the monster's grip, ramming it in the fiend's gut. The blow sent it flying up against a tree, shattering it half way up. The ogre landed on the jagged stump impaling itself. It tried to raise up on one knee then slumped as its life source ran out with its blood tainting the ground with its stench.

……………..

Ongie sat up wondering where he was and how this could be possible. The ornate metalwork at the edge of the dome held lamps which illuminated the sphere with a soft amber light. He rose to his feet as he glanced around. Somehow he had been here before. The area was sparsely furnished. A small bed and stand were on one side with a round oak table in the middle of the room. A small kitchenette sat on the other. Nowhere was there a way out of the dome. The walls showed no evidence there was ever a passageway. It ran seamlessly around the bottom of the dome.

Ongie went over to the stand. He ran his hand over the carving on the sides stopping when he came to a leather bounded beautiful book. He traced interwoven vine pattern of circles on the covers. There was a cross woven within the rings. He opened it marveling at the ancient handwritten script. The edges were gilded in gold. Each page inticed Ongie to glean from its words. He took the book over to the table and sat down to examine closer.

Ongie flipped through the book and came to an illustration of a crucifixion. A crown of thorns embedded in His forehead. His arms stretched to their limits with large nails hammered into His wrists. His torso shown signs of torture with a gaping wound in His side. His legs crossed at the ankles held to the cross with another nail piercing them. Three women lay at the foot of the cross. Ongie flipped several more pages to another illustration. This one was an angel standing by an empty tomb talking to women.

Ongie ran his finger over the delicately raised impression of the engraving. Ongie was sure the book was a copy of the Bible. However, the script was in a language beyond his ability to comprehend.

The floor gave off a tremor as a hole developed on the side of the wall. Will-O stepped through. The wall closed behind her.

"Will-O, what is this place? How is this all possible? This structure should not be able to hold back the force of the water." Ongie rose meeting her halfway. "It's as if I've been here before, but that's impossible. This place can't be real."

Will-O walked over to the table and ran her hand over the illustration before closing the Bible. She turned to Ongie as she leaned on the table. "This is real. I brought you here after Mesa Soyok Wuhti's

Katsina tried to drown you three nights ago. When it was safe, I took you back where they could find you."

"Mesa Soyok Wuhti! You are as nutty as Goyathlay. Where is the hidden door so we can get out of here? I need to find Randy." Ongie stood with his hands on his hips.

"Randy is a prisoner of Mesa Soyok Wuhti. The Katsina captured him by impersonating as the Iroquoian woman at the casino. I must prepare for battle to rescue him before she kills him."

Ongie was by her side in a flash. "You know where Randy is? Just how long have you known where he was? Are you in cahoots with this woman?" He took hold of her arm.

An arc of power jolted through Ongie's body. Ongie pulled free shaking his arm trying to stop the aching nerves from twitching. "What are you?"

Will-O pulled out the chair and pointed at it for Ongie to sit. He did so reluctantly. She drew a breath then began. "Will-O is not just my name it is also what I am. I am a Will-O'-the-Wisp. I came from the Celtic realm to the New World with your twelve times great-grandfather, Colin McGregor. I am commissioned by the Lord to protect Colin and his descendants."

Ongie shook his head. "Twelve times, that would make you….."

"Centuries old, yes. I have watched over your family for seven centuries. It was I that turned Mesa Soyok Wuhti's blade from Goyathlay's throat so many years ago. Goyathlay has given me the most trouble keeping him safe. His recklessness he took for bravery almost cost him his life."

"What, what about us? Am I just one of your charges?" Disbelief clouded Ongie's heart.

Will-O shook her head, "Our relationship has gone beyond what it is supposed to be. For the first time since the Lord appointed me guardian of your family I've allowed a relationship to go beyond concern for my charges wellbeing."

Ongie stood up and backed away. "So you are telling me what you feel for me is one of concern for a charge? You feel nothing more than what you would my grandfather?"

Will-O took a step toward Ongie only to have him back away from her. "This discussion will have to wait until I have rescued Randy. I need to know if your faith is strong enough to assist me in this or stay here while I free Randy. I had dispatched the Katsina when I rescued you from her clutches. So it is only Mesa Soyok Wuhti I have to battle to free Randy. I would prefer you release Randy while I fight her, so Randy is not hurt during the combat. We need to do this before she summons the other Katsinas to protect her. I need your answer. Do you stay here or come with me while I battle?" Will-O turned and went to the wall, waving her hand in front of the wall, opening a doorway into an armory.

She retrieved a breastplate engraved with a Celtic tree of life, belting it on then a sword belt. She then put on cuisses, poleyns, greaves, and gauntlets. Last came a helmet and sword. The sword pulsed with a light blue light as she held it in her hand. Will-O slid the sword into the scabbard as she turned back to Ongie. "I need your answer, for there is not much time left for Randy. Mesa will kill him as soon as she learns her Katsina is dead."

Ongie shook his arm one last time as he viewed the warrior standing before him. His mind kept trying to deny what it conveyed to him and wanted him to run the other way. His heart overruled the fear with his love for his friend and this warrior standing before him.

He walked over to her. "I need a weapon."

Will-O reached into the armory retrieving a carved antler handled knife, handing it to Ongie.

"Here, you dropped this in the tunnel." Then she picked up her shield.

Ongie took his knife sliding it in the sheath. "I'm ready. Lead the way."

CHAPTER 18

Mesa Soyok Wuhti grumbled as she poked the fire. The Katsina should have caught Whitehorse by now. He should not have given her that much trouble in capturing him. She glanced over at the cage hanging from the ceiling. The crumbled form laid motionless at the bottom. She wished Randy had more courage than fear quivering in his body. Bravery made the flesh more flavorful than fear. Anxiety taints the meat without a balance of boldness and makes its muscle limp.

She walked out of the longhouse glancing up at the feathery clouds crossing the sky. Suddenly a whiff of death came on the wind to her nostrils. She breathed in the rancid odor. She threw her head back howling into the wind.

The wind carried the howl for miles to a cave high in the mountains. A scruffy hand grabbed the side of the entrance heaving a massive body with it. The ogre answered the howl with one of its own. Deep within the bowels of the cave came a high whining howl echoing off the walls. A slightly smaller ogre appeared.

"What has happened that you have given the emergency howl?" The small ogre glanced around.

"Mesa Soyok Wuhti has called us to her. Something has happened to our sister."

The small ogre turned and picked up two clubs the size of small trees, handing the larger one to the other ogre. "How long will it take us to reach her?"

The other sent a howl on the wind then turned to the smaller one. "If we travel by top speed we can reach her within the hour."

....

Will-O had just stepped from the tunnel when the wind brought a whisper of a howl in it. She stopped and listened to the wail. Ongie came up behind her.

"What's wrong? Why have we stopped?"

"The wind carries the howl of Mesa Soyok Wuhti. She is calling the other Katsinas to her aid. We must hurry." She took off running.

Ongie stretched his legs as far as he could to keep Will-O in sight. The trees and bushes became a blur as they traveled through the forest. Sweat drenched Ongie's body. His jeans clung to him like a second skin. Still, Will-O did not slow her pace. Her movements reminded Ongie of a hummingbird darting around things in its path to the fullest nectar-filled flower. Not once did her foot falter between the stones and roots.

Will-O suddenly stopped causing Ongie to stumble into her as he tried to stop. She pulled him down behind a bush. Forty-three feet in front of them was an ancient palisade. The wood was worm-ridden, and leather thongs were missing in several places allowing the poles to lean severely.

Will-O placed a finger to her lips for silence as she crept forward from the bush. She slid her shield on her back as she went. At the fence, she pressed her back against the wall and peered through the leaning poles into the enclosure.

Mesa Soyok Wuhti was pacing in front of the doorway. Her knife slapped her thigh in rhythm with her steps. Mumbles of curses fell from the crooked lips. She paced over to the entrance glaring out into the forest. She went over to the tree and picked up the war club. She examined the strappings on the weapon to make sure they were still tight. Nowhere was Randy.

Will-O whispered to Ongie, "Randy must be in the longhouse. There is loose bark on the back that you should be able to pry off without alerting Mesa to your presence. Wait until I have engaged her before you go."

"No. I can't allow you to put yourself in harm's way. You rescue Randy, and I will confront Mesa." Ongie started to move around her.

She placed her hand upon his chest. "That will not work. If you confront her, she will know you are not alone. Then the element of deception will be lost. I have come up against Mesa Soyok Wuhti and her kind before while protecting your family. The Lord has provided me with the weaponry I need." She slipped to the other side of the leaning poles looking back at Ongie. "Remember to wait until I have her fully engaged before you start the rescue."

Will-O slid along the fence to the entrance. Mesa Soyok Wuhti was by the tree swinging the war club in sync with the knife in a trance to heighten her awareness. Her eyes closed as she started humming the tune in her head. She danced in circles faster with each step. The hum became howls as she cried to the wind to bring the ogres to her.

Will-O stepped forth as she drew her sword and removed her shield from her back positioning it on her forearm. The sword glowed a low blue, growing brighter the closer Will-O came to Mesa Soyok Wuhti.

Mesa stopped her dance. Her back was toward Will-O. "How dare you enter my domain. You are not wanted here. This is my domain. I say who may enter it." The scraggly head turned and looked over her shoulder. "You filth. What have you done with my Katsina?"

"I dispatched it as I will do with you. Your time to rein terror has come to an end." Will-O swung the sword in an ever-widening circle. The sword grew brighter with every revolution. She circled Mesa allowing Mesa to turn with her, so Mesa's back was towards the entrance to the longhouse.

Mesa Soyok Wuhti drew down into a crouch. Her fangs grew longer protruding from her thin lips. The knife-wielding arm drew close to her body as the war club slowly came up to face Will-O. The muscles in her legs pulled tight in anticipation of an attack.

Will-O slowed the sword bringing it forward as Mesa sprang at her with war club held high and the blade ready to sink into Will-O's heart. Will-O pared the knife as she deflected the club with the shield. She shoved Mesa away with the shield then struck with a downward blow with the sword. Mesa was barely able to turn the blade from shearing her arm from her shoulder. The heat from the sword seared her flesh.

Mesa screamed in pain as she tried to raise her arm with the knife to cut Will-O's triceps muscle to cripple her sword arm.

CHAPTER 19

Ongie ran to the side of the longhouse as the sound of clanging metal filled the compound. He carved away at the bindings holding the bark to the pole. The ancient leather gave way quickly. Soon the space was ample enough for Ongie to squeeze through. He crawled through onto the lower shelf. The opening shed a sliver of illumination on the dark interior. Ongie kept his back to the breach using the small amount of light to show the items in his way.

Ongie wormed his way through the baskets by the shelf. Ongie bumped into the oversized wicker basket tipping it over. The lid came off dumping decapitated body fragments of a man over the dirt floor. Ongie knelt to examine the parts when a low moan came from a cage hanging from the ceiling by a dead fire ring.

Ongie ran to the cage. On the floor of the cage, Ongie could just make out a huddled mass. He pulled at the restrains of the cage door. It held fast. He began cutting at the bindings. The movement started moving the cage slightly. A shriek came from the mass at the sway. Ongie reached in snagging the shirt whispering, "Randy is me, Ongie. Keep still! You don't want to alert her that I am here. I'm here to rescue you. Now stay motionless."

"Ongie, oh God, please let it be true. Ongie is it you?" Randy raised his head an inch off of his arm as he tried to focus on the image on the other side of the cage.

"Yes it's me, now keep it down."

Randy lunged at the cage door. "Get me out of here! Get me out of this nightmare! The stories are real! Mesa Soyok Wuhti is real!"

Ongie pressed his hand over Randy's mouth as Ongie put a finger to his lips for Randy to comply. The pressure on his mouth focused the fear raging in Randy's body, and he tore at the hand covering his mouth.

Ongie dropped his knife and grabbed Randy's arm. "Randy, stop. You are going to get both of us captured if you keep up. We don't have that long to get out of here. I have to get you away from here.

Will-O will not be able to keep Mesa's attention too long before she figures out the attack is bogus."

Ongie picked up the knife and wiggled the tip of the blade between the bar and the binding pushing against the bands to free the door. The knife snapped off close to the quillon. The edge stuck fast between the binding and the bar. Ongie cursed under his breath as he pulled at the small nub. When that did not work, he ran over to the shelf searching for something to replace the broken knife.

There were only different size clay jars cluttering the shelf. He twirled around in desperation. Something on the other ledge across the longhouse caught his eye. He ran over and snatched the hatchet up and was back at the cage hacking at the bindings. Sparks flew as metal clashed with the ancient fastenings. There was some unknown metal woven into the bindings.

Ongie examined the strapping to see if he was making any headway. The binding was slowly shredding under the rain of blows. He doubled his effort, and finally, the first coupling gave way. The broken blade fell to the bottom of the cage. Ongie started on the next binding below the initial one.

Randy snatched up the broken blade. He sawed at the binding on the inside as Ongie worked on the outside. Soon the second binding fell away. Ongie grabbed the bars of the door and placed his foot on the side of the cage. He pulled with all his might as Randy pushed against the door. It groaned as it moved a few inches.

The movement heightened the tension. Randy slid the toes of his boots in the bars on the floor as he coiled his body down for extra inertia and shoved as Ongie pulled again. The door gave a massive groan and slid out of the frame. It hung at a downward angle.

Randy's head and shoulder wedged in the triangular opening. He wiggled and squirmed as he pushed his other shoulder through. As it came, they heard a loud pop and Randy screamed in pain. His arm hung at an odd angle.

Ongie wrapped Randy's arm around his shoulder as he grabbed Randy under the arm and finished pulling him from the cage. He sat Randy on the dirt floor, then removed his belt fashioning a sling for Randy. Once Randy's shoulder and arm were immobilized, Ongie helped Randy to the shelving against the wall.

Randy leaned against the shelving as Ongie slid his legs out the hole in the wall. He twisted around until he was half out then reach to help Randy when Ongie disappeared with a whoosh tearing a large chunk of the wall free as he went.

Randy slid back in horror as a massive ogre's leg wedged into the opening sending everything on the shelving hurling to the floor. Randy fled from the intruding mass coming through the wall. He reached the door when he was snatched up by the back of his shirt. The ogre brought him close to its face. Its sunken black eyes squinted in the dim light as the rancid breath gagged Randy.

Randy shoved his fist into the hideous nose trying to free him from the grasp. The ogre's head drew back as it let out an enormous sneeze covering Randy in slime.

The ogre wiped its nose with the back of its hand as it shook Randy with the other. It slammed Randy against the door before kicking the door off its hinges.

Will-O Wisp

CHAPTER 20

Will-O slammed Mesa back once again with the shield as she slashed a deep gouge in Mesa's forearm. The knife clattered to the ground at Will-O's feet as Mesa backpedaled fleeing the tip of Will-O's blade. She slammed the war club against Will-O's shield trying to stop Will-O's advance. Will-O pressed on alternating use of the shield and sword to halt the war club. Mesa swung the club at Will-O's head as Will-O countered with the sword. The blade sliced through the club rendering it useless. Mesa threw the rest at Will-O and tried to flee. Will-O batted it away with the sword as she threw the shield hitting Mesa at the back of the knees. Mesa went down for an instant then clawed at a tree trunk to right herself.

Mesa hissed as the tip of Will-O's blade pinned her against the trunk of the tree. "Surrender, and I will allow you to live, Mesa. Your reign of terror has come to an end." Will-O moved the blade tip closer to Mesa to emphasize her point.

They turned towards the longhouse as the door exploded off its hinges followed by a giant ogre breaking free of the wall. Randy hung limply in its fist. The other ogre rounded the longhouse dragging Ongie by the ankle.

A raunchy laugh erupted from Mesa. "It's you that need to surrender, or I will destroy those in your care."

The ogre holding Ongie raised its arm over its head ready to bash Ongie into the chopping block. Will-O lowered her sword. Mesa sneered as she reached for the blade as the ogre swung Ongie in an arc at the block. Will-O screamed no as she ran toward the ogre. The ogre roared as a searing pain shot through its arm as the tomahawk tore through its wrist. Ongie fell to the ground inches from the chopping block.

Goyathlay stood at the palisade's gate. An arrow notched in his bow ready to follow the tomahawk. Jordyn and Sue were at his side with Julie and LaVina coming up behind them.

The other ogre grabbed Randy by the head. Randy screamed as the ogre started squeezing. A blast exploded as the .357 Ruger ripped into the ogre's shoulder from Jordyn's rifle. It dropped Randy to the ground. Sue fired her six-shooter at the ogres as they turned their anger toward the group at the gate.

Goyathlay met the charge of the one-handed ogre with a stream of arrows then drew his warclub slamming it in the ogre's chest, driving the shafts deeper into the chest muscles. Goyathlay slammed the warclub against the side of its head. The ogre roared in pain as the velocity snapped it sideways. The ogre fell to its knees. Goyathlay swung the club in an arc bringing it down on top of its head. The ogre fell forward unconscious landing with a solid thud.

Sue emptied her gun into the body of the charging ogre. "Kneecap it, Jordyn!" Sue screamed as she reloaded.

Jordyn aimed the rifle, and it exploded again. The bullet found its mark shattering the kneecap. The ogre's face plowed into the dirt. It tried to rise but the destroyed knee would not hold, and it fell holding the knee as it moaned in excruciating pain.

LaVina and Julie ran to the fallen men dragging them away from the fighting. Will-O turned back to Mesa when she saw the two women coming for the fallen men. Mesa grabbed the tomahawk before fleeing, leaving the ogres to the mercy of the group. Will-O grabbed her shield up as she pursued the fleeing adversary.

CHAPTER 21

Jordyn pointed the rifle at the moaning ogre's head ready to pull the trigger to put the fiend out of its misery. Sue reached over and pulled the gun barrel away. "No. There is no need to do that. It cannot hurt us now."

"Are you nuts? We need to destroy them while they are helpless."

"The Bible states to love your enemies and do good to those that hate you."

"The Bible also states there is a time to kill." Jordyn pointed the rifle back at the ogre. "And now seems to be that time."

LaVina laid a gentle hand on Jordyn's shoulder. "The full verse is there is a time to kill and to be killed. We are not the Lord to choose which time it is. The boys need medical attention more than we need revenge." She turned back to Ongie leaning against the gate.

Jordyn gave a humph and pulled the trigger. The bullet splattered the ogre with gravel as it cringed. "Never forget creature I gave you your miserable life. That is the only mercy you will ever get from me. Never let me see you again." She slung the rifle strap over her shoulder and placed Ongie's arm over her other shoulder.

Ongie lifted his head and glanced around the compound. "Where is Will-O? I heard her scream. Is she all right?"

Goyathlay came up taking LaVina's place. "Do not worry about Will-O, Ongie. The Lord is protecting her as she does His will. We need to get Randy and you medical help." He pulled Ongie along the trail leading away from the palisade. Julie and Sue followed with Randy in tow. Jordyn brought up the rear as she kept a vigilant eye on the gate to make sure no one followed.

CHAPTER 22

The thick gray fog swallowed the palisade as they reached the edge of the forest. It swirled around their knees making it feel like they were treading through molasses as they hurried along. At the side of the spring, it had reached their waist.

Goyathlay stabbed at the ground with his longbow to find a way across the spring. The fog sucked at the bow, trying to wrench it free of Goyathlay's grip. No matter where he attempted the bow sank beyond reach. Goyathlay shook his head. This made no sense. The spring had only been ankle deep less than an hour ago. The fog creeping up their body made Goyathlay uneasy. The coils of fog constricted across their chest. With each breath, the coils tightened restricting the air flow to their lungs.They had to make it out of the mist before it swallowed them.

Goyathlay swung the bow in the broader arc, and the bow struck something hard. Goyathlay took a deep breath then dove into the fog. They could no longer see him as the fog filled in behind him.

"Goyathlay. Goyathlay have you found a way across the stream? Goyathlay can you hear me? Goyathlay!" Jordyn swept the fog searching for him. Suddenly, something grabbed her hand and yanked sending her headfirst into the mist.

Sue grabbed the disappearing rifle giving it a jerk with all her might. Julie took Sue's arm pulling with her. Slowly Jordyn rose from the fog and Goyathlay came with her. They gasped for breath trying to cleanse their lungs from the mist.

"Cough, cough, there – there's a small stone walkway, no more than two feet wide. We will have to go single file to make it." Goyathlay cleared the rest of the fog from his lungs.

"But what about Randy and Ongie they need help walking?" Julie swatted the fog away from her face.

"I can walk now. We need to figure out about Randy."Ongie straightened up favoring his right ankle. "We can't use a sling to carry him the fog would smother him before we got across."

"Place Randy on my back I will carry him across. LaVina, you can help hold him steady. The rest of you hold on to the person in front of you so you can follow the path and help each other." Goyathlay slung Randy up awkward on his back as he wrapped Randy's arms over his shoulders.

LaVina grabbed Randy's belt helping Goyathlay center Randy's body on his back. Julie laid a hand on LaVina, Ongie came next. Jordyn tried to reach Ongie's shoulder but settled for his belt instead. Sue brought up the rear. She kept an ever watching vigil over her shoulder.

Goyathlay started across feeling his way with his foot. The stones became slimy. Each step slid sideways as the fog crept further up their bodies. Julie kept bobbing up and down trying to keep her nose above the smothering fog. Ongie reached down and snagged Julie around her waist and hauled her upon his hip as he took ahold of LaVina's shoulder with his free hand.

"Whoa, I should be carrying you not the other way around." Julie pulled back slightly.

"I'm sure you could but how long can you hold your breath?" Ongie smiled as he took a wobbly step forward.

"Point taken." Julie shook her head.

"Don't worry Julie I won't let him slip." Jordyn grabbed Ongie's belt with both hands steadying him. "We need to get going. It's up to my chin. Sue, how are you doing back there?"

"More walking and far less talking. Move it!" Sue swatted at the fog. "I think there is something in this soup. I felt something slid in between Jordan and me."

Goyathlay picked up the pace as fast as the slippery stones would allow. His foot soon felt the solid ground of the bank. The fog suddenly stuck to Goyathlay's legs like cement. It tugged down on his body and Randy, trying to yank Randy under the murkiness. Goyathlay tightened his grip on Randy as he lunged forward.

They popped free landing on the grassy bank. The fog ripped Ongie's grip loose of LaVina's shoulder. LaVina fell beside Randy. Goyathlay released Randy and scrambled back into the soup. He swung his hand wildly in search of Ongie. The mist twisted around his arms with the strength of metal bands. It crawled up his arms in its attempt to stop him.

Goyathlay fought back, flexing his muscles breaking the fog's hold as he laid down prayer after prayer. A large misshapen dark image appeared before him. He reached out grasping at the image. It grabbed his arm pulling itself towards him. Ongie's tired face came into view. Goyathlay drew Ongie to him.

Ongie gave him a quick one arm hug then handed Julie off to him. Goyathlay positioned Julie on his back then made sure Ongie had a tight hold on Julie's shoulder before he turned and headed out again. This time everyone came free of the mist.

They coughed and hacked the rest of the mist out of their lungs. They basked in the warm rays of the sun allowing its warmth to rid them of the last clinging grasp of damp. It strengthened their souls freeing them of the lingering fear that was there moments ago.

Sue turned back to find the fog was gone and babbling brook replaced the slimy stream. "What just happened? Where did that strange fog go?"

Goyathlay smiled raising his face to the sun. "We are no longer in Mesa Soyok Wuhti's domain. The darkness is no longer hanging over our land. With the Lord and the wisp's help, we have defeated Mesa's plan to enslave our people so she could feed upon us at her leisure." He pointed a warning finger at Ongie and Randy. "Remember this well. Make sure the rest of your generation knows my stories ring with truth for you have lived through this one. Guard our people well."

"Ethiso:da` why are you talking like this? We are safe. You said so yourself." Ongie started toward Goyathlay.

Goyathlay held his hand up halting him. "It is time for you to take the mantle of leadership of the False Face Society. My time as leader is at an end. I have already talked this over with Clan Mother, and she agrees with me. You are next, and Randy will be in training for the Sachems."

"Goyathlay I don't know what to say. I have dreamed all my life to be a Sachem." Randy sat up favoring his ribs.

"You have not made it yet. You have a long way to go before you are ready to be a Sachem. Clan Mother will be keeping a closer eye on you during this time, so you will not have time to be catting around our Rayen." Goyathlay reached down and pulled Randy to his feet. "First thing you need to learn is not to be ashamed of your name. Randy Greystone is no more, Naulowa Greystone is here to stay."

Randy groaned from the sudden movement. Goyathlay just shook his head then held out a hand to LaVina. "Naulowa, lead us back to the festival."

Randy glanced around as he held his ribs. After a few minutes, he started out for the village with the rest of the group falling in line behind him. Ongie and Goyathlay brought up the rear. Goyathlay allowed the team to move beyond hearing range before he turned to Ongie. "Ongie what do you know about Will-O?"

Ongie glanced up at the sky before he answered. "Ethiso:da`, this past four days I have been tossed and turned every which way but loose. How can I know if any of this is real? YEOW!"Ongie rubbed his shoulder from where Goyathlay poked him with the point of an arrow. "Why did you do that? That hurt."

"This adventure is as real as the arrow prick in your skin. Now answer my question." Goyathlay chuckled as he replaced the arrow back in the quiver.

Ongie glared down at his grandfather. "She claims to be some creature that is centuries old who is commissioned by God to protect our tribe. I don't know who's crazier her or me for even contemplating the thought what she says could be real."

"Actually it is our line that she watches over. The tribe receives the benefit of this relationship. Will-O is a wisp, not a creature. Colin McGregor came over to our lands in the early 1500's.Will-O came with him as his guardian. Once here he won the hand of Sweet Water, my eleventh great-grandmother. Will-O has watched over each generation of our family down through the centuries. Even foolish young braves with no brains they mistake for bravery like your Ethiso:da`.

"She saved my life. I am eternally grateful the Lord commissioned her to do this. A wisp usually only gives someone glimpses of what their future may be."

"So she comes and plays with our lives making us pick up the pieces of mayhem she leaves in her wake." Ongie grounded his words through clenched teeth. "Just how many of our men did she deceive with those lips of hers?

Wham! Ongie slammed to the ground from Goyathlay's fist. "Do not talk like a buffoon. Will-O is not a harlot. She takes her commission seriously as you should yours. Why do you spout such foolishness about such a crucial situation? Maybe we were wrong on you being ready to lead the False Face Society." Goyathlay shook his head and turned slowly walking away.

Ongie climbed to his feet and followed them. His soul was in a turmoil over what had transpired. How could any of this be real? His mind kept trying to convince him it had been some nightmare or hallucination. His heart said otherwise. The pain of regret from the way he talked to Will-O. What if she was not successful in her fight against Mesa Soyok Wuhti? How could he live with himself if that happened? So many thoughts and accusations ran through his mind as they finally arrived back at the village.

Clan Mother met them at the gate. She had several assistants take Randy and the authors to the first-aid station. She reached out for Ongie, but he shrugged off her advance and walked away, his head hung down in defeat. She turned to Goyathlay with an unspoken accusation on her lips.

Goyathlay wrapped an arm around her shoulder pulling her into a tight embrace before answering the unspoken question. "Ongie needs time to digest everything that has happened to him. Do not worry we have raised Ongie to be the warrior he was meant to be. Be patient my love. He will rise to the task." They went to the first-aid station to check on how Randy was doing.

The authors were still there keeping an eye on Randy's treatment. The medic was able to pop his shoulder back into place and was in the process of checking him for any other wounds.

Goyathlay laid a hand on Jordyn's shoulder. "I thank you all for your help in rescuing my grandson and his friend. I could not have done it without your help."He shook each of their hands. "I am glad that you had your firearms with you. You both are excellent marksmen, especially you Jordyn. I was amazed you could kneecap that ogre while it was running."

"As I told your grandson, we make sure we bring everything we could ever need on our trips.We need to get packed so we can arrive at our next book signing on time."

"Please remember you all have a place in my longhouse as part of my family." Clan Mother added as she pointed out the wounds the medic missed on Randy."

"Thank you, we will. This adventure has given us many scenarios for future novels." LaVina smiled as they climbed into Jordyn's van.

CHAPTER 23

Ongie went to the Niagara River each night after work for the next three weeks in search of some sign of Will-O. The only thing that met him was the rush of the water along with the roar of the falls. He meandered along the railing remembering the softness of her touch on his cheek, the way her chestnut hair fell across her face when she tried to hide what she was feeling.

He gave a deep sigh as he turned from the falls as the fog rolled in covering everything in a blanket of white. By the time he had passed the Peace Bridge the mist had drenched his clothes.

"One of these days I will not be here to keep you dry."

Ongie spun around into Will-O's arms. "Where have you been? I've looked everywhere for you. I practically gave up hope of ever seeing you again." He wrapped his arms around her waist whisking her off her feet as he sought her plush lips.

She stopped his lips with her hand before he could complete their objective. "Not here. Please let me down so we can go somewhere more private so that we can talk."

Ongie glanced about. "There is no one anywhere near us."

"Please."

He reluctantly released his hold on her waist settling for her hand instead. Will-O lead him down the river bank away from the Peace Bridge before she opened the tunnel to her dwelling. The tunnel closed behind them.

Under the dome once more, Will-O handed Ongie a towel then set about making tea. He dried off as he set at the table watching her at her task. Will-O placed a cup in front of Ongie then sat across from him. She kept her eyes on her cup as she stirred sugar into the tea.

Ongie reached across the table and took ahold of her stirring hand, making her stop. "Will-O I don't want tea. I can't eat. I can't sleep. I can't even keep my mind on my job. My mind has focused only on you. You and Ethiso:da` has spun a web of unbelievable events. He says you came over with Colin McGregor in the 1500's. Will-O, this can not be correct. That would make you over" –

"Over seven centuries old, and I am not telling just how much older. So it's my age that has you in a tailspin, that you care for someone older than you?"

"Yes, I mean no, I don't know what I mean. Will-O how can all this be true? Ethiso:da` says you're the guardian of our family all these years yet you look to be my sister's age. I need to straighten things out in my head and heart. Just what is a wisp anyway?"

Will-O stood a deep sigh escaped her lips as she began to pace. "A wisp is a member of the fairy realm. Most wisps give humans glimpses of the near future. The Lord gives a rare few like me special commissions. I have watched over your family for many generations before Colin's wild adventurous nature took him from his homeland to come to America. I guarded him making sure he did not fall overboard in the storms trying to drown him. I keep an eye on him as he fell head over heels in love with Sweet Water then had to convince her mother he was worthy of her daughter.

"Each generation brought new trails and adventures in keeping the wonder lust ones safe. Then Goyathlay went to Arizona to visit friends. There Mesa Soyok Wuhti found him and has plagued the tribe ever since. It was she that caused the truck to overturn killing your parents when you were a mere child. She sought your life even back then. Her grip on this realm was not that strong, and I was able to stop her, sending her back to her realm. I carried you back to your grandparents, giving you to them and relayed the sad news of your parents' death. I reassured them they were not within Mesa's clutches."

"You watched me grow up?"

Will-O smiled, "I was there watching over you as your mother gave you life, listened as Goyathlay talked her into allowing him to name you. From the moment you took your first breath, I felt the surge in your soul. It was even stronger than your grandfather's soul. Dwelling within you is the last strain Celtic genes from your grandfather Colin."

"What about Rayen? She's my sister so she should also have Celtic genes."

"She is your sister however children do not receive the same genes. It is a mixture of the parents' genes, and each child is unique. Siblings only posses twenty-five percent of the same gene sequences from the parents. Rayen did not receive the Celtic genes."

Ongie got to his feet and snagged her in midstride. "What does all this talk about genes have to do with us?"

Will-O hung her head. "It has everything to do with it. I am the guardian of Colin McGregor's line. It stops with you unless you pass the genes down to your children. Ongie I am a wisp. I can not have your children no matter how much I want it."

"Then so be it. Let the line die with me as long as we can be together." He tried to draw her to him.

"Would you take away the extra protection from Rayen and Naulowa's children?" She held him at bay with a hand against his chest.

"Children? Rayen is pregnant with Randy's baby?" Ongie's brow drew down. "I'll beat him to a pulp."

"No. Rayen is not pregnant yet. I have seen their future. They are destined to lead your tribe. My commission is finished if you die without having children, and I will be no more. I have lived longer than most wisps. My commission is my life. I must not hold you to the love you carry for me. Your love must turn to another for the safety of your tribe."

Ongie crushed her to his chest. "But I want no other. You are what I want and need. Why can't I love you? I have never wanted or needed anything like my love for you."

Will-O returned his embrace. "I know for the same love burns within my soul. The thought of allowing this love turn to another is tearing my soul apart. But I cannot be selfish for I have seen what can come from giving you up and I cannot deny you the joy you will feel when you hold your first born and the love of the child's mother." She pulled away. "By doing this, I will still be able to watch over you and your descendants. I can be happy knowing that you will be loved."

He grabbed her by the arms. "Will-O I meant what I said. I want no other one but you. You are my heart and soul."

She pulled away. Tears streamed down her face. "If you truly love me you will do what I say."

"Will-O," he reached for her and stumbled to the ground next to the railing by the falls. "NOOOOO!" The anguish tore at his soul as his heart fell. "WILL-O! NO! DON'T DO THIS TO US! WILL-O!"

CHAPTER 24

Ongie coiled the thick rope then stored it in the locker. He waved a hand to the crew as he disembarked from the boat. He shoved his hands deep into his pockets as he slowly climbed the stairs. Goyathlay waited at the top of the stairs leaning against the railing watching Ongie approach.

When Ongie reached the landing, Goyathlay fell in step alongside his grandson. They walked silently to Ongie's truck. They climbed in, and Ongie turned the key. The only sound that met their ears was clicking. Ongie groaned as he gripped the steering wheel yanking back and forth. "Why is it everytime you want to talk to me you sabotage my truck?"

Goyathlay chuckled, "This way we have time to talk as you figure out what is wrong with the truck."

Ongie twisted in the seat, resting his arms on the steering wheel and the back of the bench. "How about we just forgo the theatrics and get down to what you want to know?"

"Why are you still moping? Our tribe no longer is under the curse of Mesa Soyok Wuhti."

"Why are you so nosey? I'm fine. Everything is just fine. The sun is shining. The flowers couldn't be more exquisite. Everything is right with the world."

"If that is so then why are you moping? Your face is longer than a giraffe's neck. You no longer go out on dates. There is no joy in your eyes. It is as if your soul has died and forgot to take you with it."

"Ethiso:da` please just let it lie. Tell me what you did to the truck so we can go home." Ongie turned back around placing his hand over his mouth and chin.

"No."

"No?" Ongie's head snapped to the side.

"No. Aarushi says I can not come home until I make it right with you." Goyathlay crossed his arms, leaned back and closed his eyes.

Ongie groaned, "Ethiso:da`, you can tell Grandmother everything is fine between us. There was never anything wrong in our relationship."

Goyathlay did not move. Ongie began to think he fell asleep. Ongie climbed out of the cab and lifted the hood to see if he could locate what Goyathlay did to the truck. After two hours Ongie gave up and went around to the passager side of the truck. He rapped on the window with his knuckle. Goyathlay rolled the window down. A blank stare greeted Ongie.

"Okay, I give up. Walk with me." Ongie turned walking away without an answer.

Goyathlay's steps fell in line with Ongie. They walked along the railing for the length of the island before Ongie stopped and leaned on the fence. Goyathlay stood silently beside him for an hour.

"Ethiso:da` how can I stop loving her? How can I love someone else with my heart torn out of my chest? There is nothing but pitch in my soul. Have you ever loved someone but they threw your love back in your face?"

"Ongie did Will-O throw your love away? This I can not believe." Goyathlay laid a hand gently on Ongie's back.

"She said our love could not be, that I should love someone that could give me children. I told her I did not care if I had children, only that I loved her. But she scorned my love and threw me back on the riverbank. I have not heard or seen her since."

"Ongie before I answer your questions, answer me this, Do you love me?"

"Of course I do."

"Do you love Grandmother and Rayen?"

"Yes, these are redundant questions, Ethiso:da`."

"Did your love for me stop when you first loved Rayen?"

"NO, Ethiso:da` I still love you as much as I ever did but these questions are trying my patience. Please just get to the point."

"I have already answered your questions with your answers. Do not try to divide your love or compartmentalize it. Allow the Lord to multiply your love. I saw the love Will-O had for you when she brought you to us so many years ago. She has and always will love and watch over you. Come we need to go home before Aarushi sends the whole tribe out after us." Goyathlay turned toward the parking lot.

"Errr, Ethiso:da`, the truck, what did you do to it?"

Goyathlay reached deep into his pocket rummaging around then pulled out the rotor handing it back to Ongie then continued on his way chuckling as he went. Ongie drew a deep breath his mouth twisting into a smirk as he followed his grandfather.

From the mist, Will-O watched them leave. She kissed her fingertips and gently blew a kiss on the breeze to Ongie.

Ongie looked around as the kiss landed on his cheek seeing only the mist. He rubbed his cheek as he turned and followed Goyathlay to the truck. He replaced the rotor and closed the hood. Ongie glanced at the river one last time before he climbed in, started the vehicle and took off.

A stream of tears coursed down her cheeks as the taillights disappeared into the mist.

ABOUT THE AUTHOR

Sue Raymond was born and raised in the Midwest along with her siblings. Sue was trained in the Commercial Art field before marrying her husband. After raising two sons and having five grandchildren Sue started a new avenue in her life, writing. She has nine published novels as she works on four other novels and children's stories.

Future titles in the works:

Grampa's House Needs Painting

Seeds of Chance

The Muddy Seed

A Sled Ride with Daddy

A Snowy Seed of Love

Healer of Surflex Color book

The Rose Competition

Sudan Terror